In the Ghost Detective Universe:

Novels
(Best to be read in order)
Beyond the Grave
Unveiling the Past
Beneath the Surface

Short Stories
(All stand-alone)
Just Desserts
Lost Friends
Family Bonds
Common Ground
Till Death
Family History
Heritage
Eternal Bond
New Beginnings
Severed Ties

R.W. WALLACE

Author of the Tolosa Mystery Series

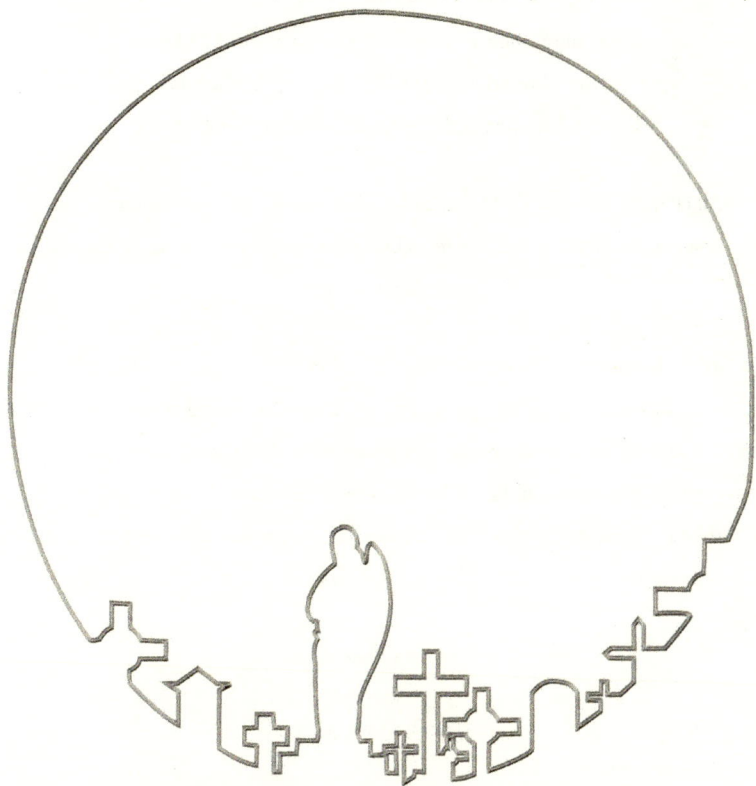

BEYOND the GRAVE

Book 1 of the Ghost Detective Series

Beyond the Grave
by R.W. Wallace

Copyright © 2021 by R.W. Wallace

Copy editing by Wendy Janes
Cover by the author
Cover Illustration 10926765 © germanjames | 123rf.com
Cover Illustration 193142734 © pyty | Adobe Stock
Cover Illustration 263199440 © Nouman | Adobe Stock

www.rwwallace.com

ISBN: [979-10-95707-58-5]

Main category—Fiction
Other category—Mystery

First Edition

Welcome to my Ghost Detective books. I've been living with these characters in my head for a while, and a certain number of stories have come out of it. So many, in fact, that there are two parallel timelines.

A quick word to explain.

I started writing short stories about Robert and Clothilde. Had *so* much fun with them. And wondered what had happened to them when they died. They stayed so secretive! Then came the story *Common Ground*, and I got a definite link to Clothilde. And a way to get them out of the cemetery!

"Cool!" I thought, and started writing the next short story. Which wasn't a short at all, but rather the beginning of a series of novels, the first of which you're holding right now.

But I didn't want to stop writing the shorts. So I've done both. In one timeline (this one), the ghosts get out of the cemetery and go looking for their own murderers, and in the other (the shorts), they're still stuck in the cemetery and helping other ghosts find peace.

All of that to say you definitely do not need to read the short stories before starting the novels (though *Common Ground* will give some extra background), and the shorts can be read in any order. The novels, however, are best read in order.

Enjoy!

R. W. Wallace

ONE

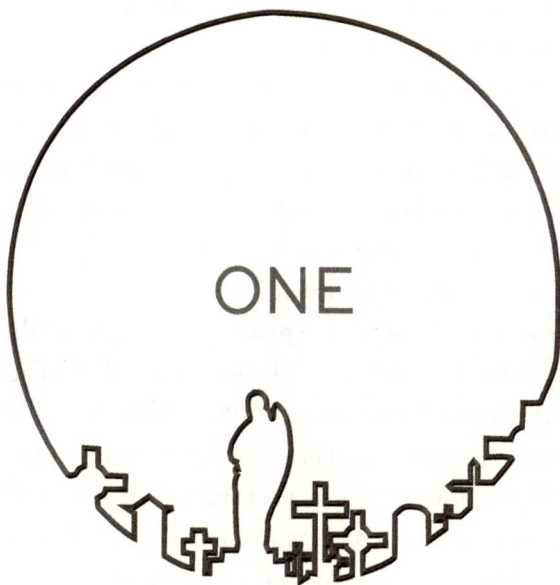

GHOSTS ARE NOTHING but people who died with unfinished business. Once the business is dealt with, they move on to the afterlife.

Sounds easy enough, right?

Wrong.

Ghosts are also bound to the cemetery they are buried in, unable to escape their confines. Which means that unless the person associated with the unfinished business shows up in the cemetery, the business stays unfinished.

Even when the person does show up in the cemetery, there's no guarantee we can accomplish our mission. Our interactions with the world of the living are severely limited—although not non-existent—and we often have to get creative.

For the most part, we manage.

My friend Clothilde and I have haunted this cemetery for over thirty years and we've helped countless ghosts move on to the afterlife. Murders have been solved, spouses have been forgiven, family secrets have been unearthed. It's become our mission in death to help others move on.

And yet, the two of us remain.

Our graves are close to the squeaking back gate of the small cemetery, with the gray stone wall outlining our field of action at our backs, the small stone church with its bronze spire and large wooden doors at the far end of the cemetery straight ahead, and gray tombstones and mausoleums covering the rest of the area. Some graves are simple and understated like Clothilde's, some are more like palaces with columns and spires and crying angels, while yet others used to be grand but have long since fallen into disrepair and barely show the name of the person who was buried there decades or centuries ago.

There's a certain ebb and flow to the life in a cemetery.

Some days, especially in winter, we won't get a single visitor. The church doors stay closed, the back gate remains silent, and the small parking lot stays empty. When the gray clouds of a southern French winter lay so low we can barely see the top of the church spire, the sounds become muffled, making us wonder if the world of the living is still out there, and water clings to the dark granite of the tombs and runs down the faces of the sculpted angels, letting them shed real tears.

When the sun bears down on us the hardest in summer, the elderly visitors wisely stay away. There's some shade under the plane trees lining the main path or under the large cedar tree, but mostly, the graves absorb the sunlight and send it back to our visitors ten-fold, making a visit to our cemetery a stifling experience. If there's any wind, it's blocked by the wall or the larger mausoleums. Only the most desperate will show up on a day like that.

Other than the obvious crowd for the Day of the Dead in November, we get the most visitors in spring. The temperature is in the agreeable twenties, the sun makes a first appearance after months of hiding behind clouds, and nature is waking up and reminding people that they are alive.

This quite often translates into thinking about the dead, and wanting to bring some life to the graves of their loved ones. So, in addition to all the flowers growing naturally in our cemetery, graves receive roses and daffodils, lilies and tulips. Our cemetery becomes the canvas for the most colorful of flower arrangements.

No flowers have ever graced my grave, or that of Clothilde, because in thirty years, we haven't had a single visitor.

In my case, this makes sense. After all, the only thing marking my grave is a slight bump in the ground next to Clothilde's tomb-stone, which shows how much—or rather how little—anybody cared about my demise.

I can't say I blame them. The reason I'm still here as a ghost thirty years after my death, after all, is because I have sins to atone for before I can move on to the afterlife. I was a lousy police officer, a lousy brother, and a terrible son.

I wouldn't want to honor my memory, either.

I made my peace with the status quo a long time ago, in large part because I've found a way to work toward a possible redemption. If I solve enough crimes, help enough ghosts, perhaps I can make up for the crimes I didn't solve while I was alive, the people I didn't help.

For Clothilde, the fact that she hasn't had a single visitor makes a lot less sense.

She arrived as a ghost in this cemetery in the late eighties, a few short weeks before my own death, and has hung around here ever since, being my friend but sharing little to nothing about her past. She was twenty years old when she died and will forever be the rebellious teenager. She's moody, mistrustful, and has a terrifically dry sense of humor. She loves perching on tombstones, with her hands under her jeans-clad thighs, and her Converse-covered feet swinging through the stone, completely ignoring the rules of the physical realm.

Her gravestone only has her name and her date of death. No date of birth. No last name.

And yet, every five years or so, a gardener comes to clean the tombstone, removing moss and weeds and repainting the gold of the engraved letters if needed.

I tried asking Clothilde if she knew who paid for this service, but she never answered.

I don't think she knows, either.

Although I guess it would make sense that it was her uncle, who apparently was the one to pay for and arrange her funeral. Not that the man has ever set foot in our cemetery.

Her mother certainly didn't have anything to do with her daughter's final resting place. She came through here as a ghost a few months ago, and was surprised to discover her daughter was in the same cemetery.

Today, a rainy April morning, Clothilde has her very first visitor.

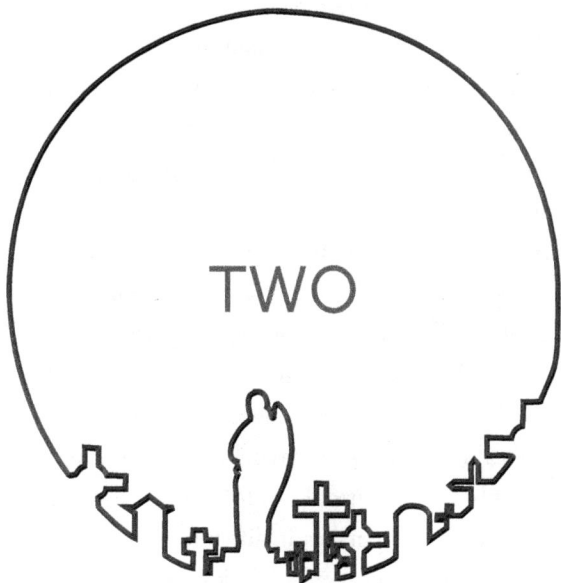

TWO

THE MAN MUST be at least seventy years old, possibly eighty. He arrives in an old and battered Renault R19 that sounds like it's on its last breath. Ignoring the downpour, he shuffles to the trunk of the car, gives it a whack to get it open, and pulls out a threadbare leather jacket. A black umbrella follows, then a bouquet of red roses.

"Haven't seen him before," I comment to Clothilde as we linger around the gate. "Wonder who the flowers are for."

Clothilde doesn't answer. She chews her lip as she studies the man, a frown marring her forehead.

Moody today, then.

Fits well enough with the atmosphere of our cemetery on a day like this. The clouds obscure the church spire and the contours of the neighboring houses look like a sulky artist's lazy take on a ghost town through the rain and fog. Only Madame Guillamot's living room window lights up like a beacon down the street.

To the north, the copse of trees separating us from the elementary school is a black hole promising an endless walk into dark eternity for anyone attempting escape. The children should be arriving at school in about an hour and their joyous screams will break the spell like a bubble bursting when poked with a toddler's finger, but it's difficult to imagine at the moment.

I've lived as a ghost in this village cemetery for thirty years and it's only logical that it ends up having an effect on me eventually. When you only see dead people and the living coming to mourn their lost loved ones, it makes it difficult to maintain any kind of sense of humor, except a rather dark one. I seem to remember that I loved a good laugh and the occasional clownery when I was alive but I remember the images more than I remember the accompanying feeling.

One feeling I haven't lost track of is the guilt. I might not have deserved to die when I did but I was no saint. I was on the verge of coming to this realization before I was killed, even got so far as to thinking I might need to make amends.

But I never got the time.

And making amends when you're a ghost stuck in a cemetery isn't exactly easy. If I can't meet or communicate with the people I wronged, it's kind of difficult to help them.

So I help the people who cross my path instead. More specifically: the ghosts who cross my path.

The only ones I haven't been able to help move on are Clothilde and yours truly. Clothilde because she's never wanted to tell me much about why she's still here and me because I honestly don't know what I need.

Also, I'd really like to make sure Clothilde is all right and not leave her here all alone. Being the only permanent ghosts for thirty years forges a certain bond.

And right now, Clothilde is one hundred percent focused on the old man approaching the cemetery.

He takes his time, his feet hardly lifting off the ground with each step, but his determination is clear.

He passes through the gate, takes a quick look around, and turns down the path running along the wall.

"There aren't any new graves that way," I comment. "Odd that we haven't seen him before, don't you think?"

Clothilde doesn't answer, of course. But her gaze is particularly intense as she walks right in front of the man, studying his face.

"Have *you* seen him before?" I ask.

The man shuffles forward. Clothilde stays just ahead.

Guess the communications will be one-sided.

Only when the old man picks the path toward the back gate does the idea take root in my mind.

"Is he coming to visit *you*, Clothilde?"

When she still doesn't answer, I step closer to the man to study his features, searching for any resemblance to my friend. But despite having been a police officer while I was alive, I'm unable to find similarities between the sagging cheeks, large nose, and high forehead of the old man, and the fresh face, sharp nose, and voluminous wavy hair of my friend.

The old man comes to a stop—in front of Clothilde's tombstone.

"Who is he, Clothilde?"

7

Slowly, and clearly with a lot of pain in the joints, the man kneels on the ground and gingerly places the roses on the fresh and wet grass.

"I'm sorry I haven't come by before, *ma chérie*," the old man says, petting the petals of the largest of the red roses. "I'd say I didn't want anyone to find you, but that is only a silly excuse I've told myself for thirty years." He gulps and closes his eyes.

"Clothilde," I say, my voice sharp. "Who is he?"

Her face is perfectly still, like that of a doll, no emotions showing. Except in the eyes. You have to know her well to be able to read her emotions, but I've lived with her and her lack of verbal cues for three decades, so I most definitely qualify.

She's scared. Angry. And sad, I think.

"Who is he, Clothilde?"

She wets her lips, something I haven't seen her do since she stopped paying attention to the rules of the physical realm and the needs of her long-lost living body.

"My uncle," she whispers.

I remember the short time while her mother had been with us as a ghost. "The one your mother asked to handle the funeral arrangements?"

Clothilde nods.

I study the old man on his knees before us. His eyes are watery and his breath short.

"Why is he here now?" I wonder out loud. "Do you think he's dying and wanted to make one last visit?"

"First visit." Clothilde's expression still hasn't changed.

She isn't going to be much help here and I'm not about to pass up an opportunity to better understand the circumstances of Clothilde's death. I want to help her find closure, so she can move on.

I kneel down next to the old man and put a hand on his shoulder. He won't be able to feel me physically, but we can often get through to people's subconscious and it works better if we touch them.

"Why are you here, old man?" I ask him. "You might feel better if you talk to her."

Clothilde's eyes flash to mine, anger burning.

"Don't you start," I tell her, keeping my voice stern. "I know you don't like to share your past, but you can't hang around here as a ghost forever. You deserve to move on just like everybody else." I nod toward her uncle. "He could help."

She grinds her teeth—another habit I haven't seen in a good twenty-five years—but keeps her mouth shut.

"What's his name?" I ask.

"Lucien," she reluctantly replies.

I focus all my attention on the old man. "Tell me, Lucien, why did you come here today?"

Lucien heaves a great breath. Lets it out slowly. His umbrella hangs limply over his shoulder, covering most of him as he kneels in the wet grass, but his left shoulder will get soaked rapidly.

"A lady came to see me yesterday," he says, his eyes on Clothilde's name on the tombstone. "A police officer named Evian. Said they were looking into cold cases and she had questions about your death."

I dare to spare a quick glance at Clothilde, but her face has completely shut down, eyes included.

Evian is the police officer we met a few weeks ago. She'd been sent down here from Paris to look into the deaths of several young women where the police work had been particularly sloppy. Two of them were ghosts in our cemetery.

Being the police officer who'd declared Clothilde's death as suicide and not murder, I know for a fact that her death qualified.

Could she be looking into older cases, too, like I'd hoped?

"She'd tried contacting your parents first, naturally," Lucien continues. "But your mother passed only a couple of months ago, and your father has been in a nursing home for several years already, his mind lost to Alzheimer's. So she found me."

He lowers his chin to his chest. "At first, I didn't want to tell her where you were buried. There was such chaos when you died. Your parents were afraid people would disturb your grave, make a spectacle. And some rather unsavory chaps came by two days after you died, while your body was still at the morgue, and wanted to look at the body. Just because.

"Your mother was beside herself with grief and worry, and was afraid she'd end up caving if they insisted, so she asked me to arrange the funeral, take care of everything." He runs a wrinkled hand down his face, his fatigue evident.

"I planned for the entire family to be invited, to do it properly. Then, when I called your mother to tell her which cemetery I'd chosen, I ended up not telling her because the scandal of your apparent suicide and the links to the City Council had just broken."

Lucien takes a deep breath and straightens his spine. "I think that's when we lost your mother, all of us. She lost her baby, her reputation, her husband's career…all in one go. So I was the only one to attend your funeral. I decided not to put your last name on the tombstone, to protect you. And I never came to visit, for fear that someone might follow me."

A tear escapes and trails down along his large nose, into the furrow running from nose to mouth, and disappears between his lips. "I apologize for that last part, *ma chérie*. It was pure cowardice on my part."

He falls silent and we all sit there for several minutes, while the rain falls down on Lucien's umbrella and the back of his coat and trousers.

I don't know what to say. Not sure if I *should* say anything.

In the end, Clothilde is the one to break the silence with a whispered question. "What is Evian going to do?"

Lucien seems to wake up from a stupor and blinks as he takes in the cemetery around us and his soaked-through left shoulder and trousers. "I wanted to see where you'd been all this time. Before all hell breaks loose again." He takes a deep breath.

"They're coming to exhume you tomorrow morning."

THREE

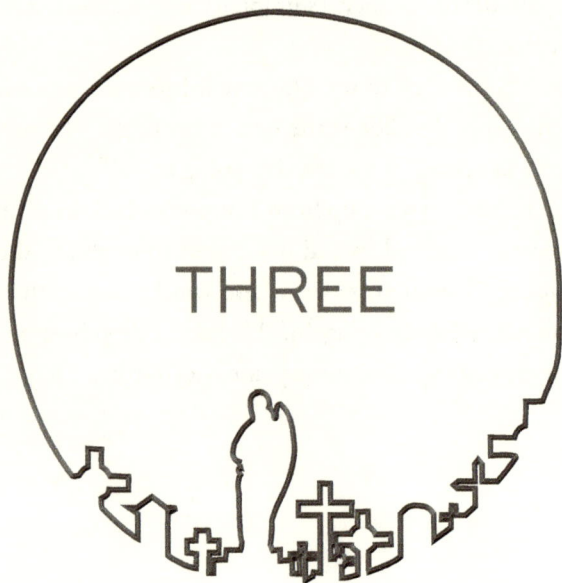

WE'VE SEEN EACH other every day for thirty years. And every night, since ghosts don't sleep.

At times we've had company, other ghosts passing through as they wrap up their unfinished business, but none who stayed for more than a few months.

She's my only friend, only companion.

And when the diggers come to exhume her, she'll go with the casket.

I'll be all alone.

But—and this is a very important but—she will have the possibility to help with making sure the people responsible for her death will be punished, and that will be worth a little loneliness on my part.

She'll actually get to leave the cemetery, something we thought impossible until two young women were exhumed not too long ago. Also done by Evian, by the way, and it seems likely their killers were the same ones who were behind Clothilde's demise.

Evian has one hell of a case on her hands.

From what I saw of her when she came to exhume our friends Lise and Manon not so long ago—and the way she solved the case, along with four others—I'm sure she's the right woman for the job. She has that no-nonsense feel about her that makes me sure she'll do whatever necessary to solve the case. The fact that she's already put one police officer behind bars on this case shows she's not afraid to ruffle a few feathers.

I just wish I could ruffle those feathers with her.

As promised, not long after the sun crests the horizon, the parking lot fills up. One police car—Evian and her young colleague I still don't know the name of—one hearse, and one tiny lorry belonging to the gravediggers.

Clothilde hasn't said much since yesterday, clearly too nervous to be either talkative or moody. She's biting her nails and running her hands through her unruly hair, yet more nervous gestures I haven't seen since our very first year together.

The diggers get to work while Evian stands at parade rest next to Clothilde's tombstone. Her young colleague follows her example. He has clearly decided she's a good role model and will copy whatever she does to learn the ropes of the job. I'd say he'll go far—so long as this case doesn't blow up and take everybody's careers with them as collateral damage.

"I guess this is it, then," Clothilde finally says as the first mound of dirt is dug up.

13

My heart lifts to see she's going to say goodbye after all. "Guess so," I reply.

"I'll probably be back in no time," she says. "Lise and Manon didn't stay away for long when they were exhumed."

"True." I nod. "But take any opportunity you find to help them find the guys who killed you, you hear me? If you get the chance to move on, you take it."

She chews her lip as she glances around the cemetery. "You'll be all alone here."

I shrug. "Don't sweat it. There are new arrivals all the time. And hey, if there's someone I really like, I'll omit to tell them they need to wrap things up in order to move on." I wink to show her I'm joking.

She chuckles nervously. Clears her throat.

And throws her arms around me.

My first ever hug from Clothilde.

"Figure out how to even out your guilt, will you?" she says in my ear. "You've done so much good here. You deserve to move on, too."

I have nothing to say to that, so I simply nod and hug her back.

It's not like I'm the one to decide when I've undone all the wrongs I did while I was alive.

A hollow *thud* sounds. Clothilde jumps and shivers.

"Casket," one of the diggers yells.

"Jeez, that's creepy," Clothilde says. "I felt that in my *bones*."

"You don't have bones."

"*Exactly!* Creepy."

Stepping forward and looking into the hole, I see they've unearthed the bottom quarter of the casket already. I think it must have been white originally, but thirty years in the ground takes a certain toll.

"Looks like your uncle got you a pretty—"

Another *thud*. This time it's my turn to shudder as my entire being is rattled from the inside out. "What the—?"

"Guys!" a tall dark-haired digger yells. "I, uh…I got another one."

Officer Evian leans forward to look into the hole. "Another what?"

"Uh…" The man scratches his head, leaving his hair full of fresh dirt. "A casket?"

Evian's voice has a brooks-no-nonsense tone. "There's a second casket?"

Clothilde and I share a glance, then jump down into the pit to have a look.

Indeed, only a centimeter or two from Clothilde's white casket, a dark brown wooden box juts out of the black dirt. It's not white or pretty like Clothilde's, but even only seeing this little of it, it does seem to be a casket.

The way I felt when the guy hit it with his shovel kind of confirms it, anyway.

"Never knew we were *that* close," I quip as I fight a smile from breaking out.

Clothilde huffs. "Really? You think this is the right place and time?"

I fight my lips into a straight line. And make the mistake of meeting Clothilde's gaze.

We break into peals of laughter, hours of stress and excitement turning into manic glee. We hold onto each other, ghost tears breaking out of our eyes and the memory of muscle cramps tearing at our stomachs.

The living people around us shift around uneasily, looking at each other, not understanding why they feel so weird all of a sudden.

"There shouldn't be a second casket down there," Evian says. She points to a gangly woman who came in the gravediggers' lorry. "Should there be a grave so close to this one? I don't see a tombstone."

That's because I never got one.

"Yeah, they're not going to find any paperwork for your grave," Clothilde says calmly.

"What?"

Her eyes meets mine. "Oh, shit. Did I never tell you that?" She glances at my casket and her mouth opens in an O.

"Tell me what, Clothilde?" The laughter is completely gone from my voice.

A hand to her cheek, the truth tumbles out. "They came in the middle of the night. Three guys, all wearing masks and not saying a word while they worked. They dug down right next to my slot—even hit my casket at one point—dropped your casket in, and closed the whole thing up. Even brought in some sort of mat of grass to put on top, to make it look undisturbed."

My mouth is hanging open. "So *nobody* knows where I'm buried?"

"Except those three guys, no."

At first I'm angry at her for not telling me, but as I take a mental deep breath, I think it through and realize it wouldn't actually have changed anything to know. Except possibly to feel even *more* stressed out about the situation I'd left behind when dying.

In the living realm, the gangly lady has her nose in some sort of screen. "I don't see anything," she says. "There's not supposed to be anybody else here. And it's against regulations to have an unmarked grave.

Mouth set in a severe line, Evian studies everybody present. "Dig it out, too," she finally says. "And none of you mention this to *anybody*."

Nods all around, and the diggers go back to work.

We stay in the pit to watch as our caskets are dug out. Shivering with every shovel hitting wood.

"Looks like you're going on an excursion, too," Clothilde says, her eyes distant.

"Looks like it."

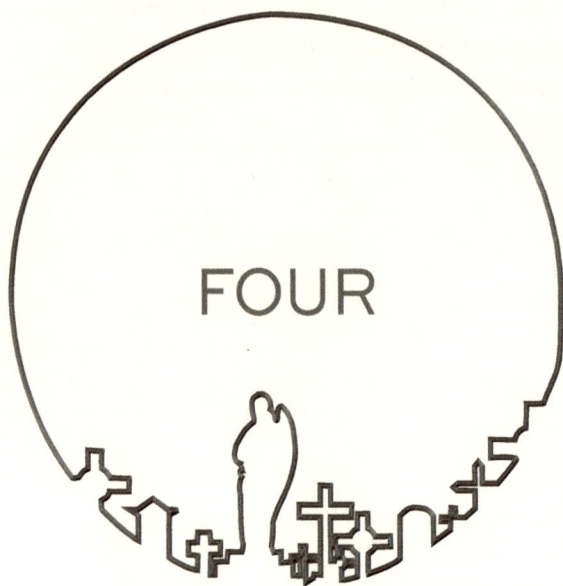

FOUR

EMELINE EVIAN STARES at the additional brown casket, willing it to give up its secrets.

She was sent to Toulouse from Paris to look into the potential murder of two young women. A quick search showed that the two women from this graveyard were not isolated cases, and Emeline got to open no less than forty cases that were open and closed as suicides by less-than-conscientious police officers in the past.

When Emeline had come back to the graveyard to make sure the two original girls—Lise and Manon—were respectfully put back in the ground, she'd somehow had the idea to look into similar cases going back thirty years.

And now, while exhuming one Clothilde Humbert, who apparently killed herself in a hotel room in 1988, here is an unexpected casket. No headstone, no trace in the administrative files, no sign of anyone having cared enough to pay for a decent casket.

Will there never be an end to the surprises on this case?

Emeline has already informed her superior in Paris that the case will take a lot longer than planned. After two weeks in a hotel room, she's tired of spending her evenings sitting on her bed and watching TV, eating takeout in her bed alone, and never feeling like she's quite in private. So she put in a request for funds to rent an actual apartment. If she stays over a month—which seems highly likely at the moment—the price will be a lot easier on the taxpayers' money than the current solution.

She's supposed to look at a cute one-bedroom near Jeanne d'Arc this afternoon—unless this Monsieur X turns out to be too interesting.

A prickling at the back of her neck makes Emeline turn to look behind her.

Nobody there.

Emeline shrugs off the feeling. Too early on a case to be seeing things that aren't there.

She eyes all the people present. She needs them to stay quiet about this second grave—and would love for them not to blab about Clothilde either. There's something special about this girl. A reason why she was buried in a place only her uncle knew about and with nothing but a first name and a date of death on the headstone.

The administrator of the cemetery shouldn't be a problem. She seems annoyed as hell that there's an extra body she didn't know about in her cemetery and will not wish for the information to get leaked. Still, Emeline will have a word with the woman before they part ways.

Malik Doubira, Emeline's young and impressionable partner, should know how to stay quiet. It's part of the job description, after all, and if Emeline is reading him right, he's looking at her with a healthy dose of hero worship, so getting him to do her bidding for a good cause won't be a problem.

The problem is with the gravediggers. There are two of them and they seem to be used to working together, never getting in each other's way and anticipating when their colleague needs more space for certain maneuvers.

They haven't said much to show they find it unusual to find two caskets where they were expecting only one but they have to be thinking it. The question is, will they talk about it amongst themselves in a "huh, that was weird" kind of way? Will they tell their significant others tonight, making it sound like this huge excitement they had at work today? Will they know it's weird enough that the papers would be interested in the story if they knew about it?

Emeline *could* attempt to order them—a second time—not to say anything. They might even listen. But it would also underline to them the importance of the find.

If she doesn't say anything more and pretends like this is no big deal, maybe they will, too.

Emeline thinks she sees movement out of the corner of her eye and turns to look. Nothing.

She always gets this way in cemeteries. Probably because it's the kind of place that's eerily quiet and brings images of slasher movies and gangly animated skeletons.

She suspects she isn't the only one to feel it. One of the diggers, a stocky man in his forties with a full mop of graying hair and the beginnings of a potbelly, stands up and looks around, one hand clenching and unclenching on the handle of his spade.

"Look alive, Vincent," his colleague tells him, not unkindly. "Don't forget there's another one after this one."

Vincent shakes his head as if trying to get rid of something, then bends back down to continue working. "Who cares if there's one or two," he mumbles. "As long as I get paid, I don't care."

Perfect. Emeline decides to go with the not-saying-anything-more-about-it option. Adults aren't that different from kids; tell them they can't do something and it's the only thing they'll want to do. Tell them nothing and they won't even realize there was something they could have potentially done.

Forty-five minutes later, both caskets are on the path and the mound of dirt has been shoveled back into the grave. Normally, they would have left the mound of dirt but Emeline didn't want anyone to be able to see, from the size of the hole, that there had been more than one casket.

"Will they both fit in the hearse?" Malik asks, his dark eyes going from the long, black vehicle in the parking lot to the two caskets—one mostly white and regal, the other no more than a wooden box.

Maybe there won't even be a body in there.

No, Emeline feels certain there's a body. And she knows she doesn't want to open it here, in front of so many witnesses. "We'll make them fit," she says. Asking for a second hearse would draw too much attention.

As the caskets are carried out of the cemetery, Emeline takes a look around. Several hundred graves, some small and decrepit with washed-out names and dates and some closer to monuments, depicting angels praying and mothers crying. The church is a classic construct for a small village in this area, with its spire barely taller than the trees of the neighboring forest.

There could be worse places to spend eternity.

"But right now," Emeline says in direction of the caskets, "I'm taking you on an excursion into the city. I've only known Toulouse for a few weeks, but I'm sure lots has changed since you last saw it thirty years ago."

FIVE

"Is that the Ponts Jumeaux? No way!" Clothilde sits on the lap of the hearse's co-pilot, a dour woman in her late fifties or sixties who hasn't said a word since we got here, but sends frequent dark looks at her colleague, probably for accepting to squeeze two coffins instead of one into the space in the back.

Clothilde hasn't spared the woman a glance since she settled in and is treating her much like she did the tombstones back in the cemetery—accepting she's there to have something to sit on but letting her feet go right through woman and car seat alike.

The usual teenager I'm-not-interested-in-anything attitude is nowhere to be seen, though. She's had her nose glued to the passenger window since we pulled out of the cemetery parking lot.

During the very short trip from the cemetery gate to the hearse, I was able to move away from the casket for quite some distance. I didn't try to go too far, because I wanted to follow Evian and our bodies to wherever she was taking us. However, the moment the doors closed on the hearse, we were stuck inside.

I'm guessing we'll always be contained wherever our bodies are contained.

A subject to be explored later because I do believe Clothilde is right; we're driving past the Ponts Jumeaux. "That's definitely the Canal du Midi," I reply to her from my seat right on top of the center console. "The three bridges and three canals are the same as the last time I came here to arrest drunkards and junkies."

The esplanade around the water has been spruced up since I last saw it, though. The construction of the highway circling Toulouse that was finished right before I died is…still there, cars speeding in all directions where there used to be small houses and a large rugby stadium.

As the hearse turns right along the Canal de Brienne, I see the industrial area on the left has become *dozens* of six-to-eight-floor apartment buildings, all perfectly aligned in a decidedly non-French manner.

I gape as we take the Catalan bridge across the Garonne toward the left bank and drive down the wide Allées Charles de Fitte. Apartment buildings have popped up everywhere. Most of them are covered in red bricks, staying on brand for Toulouse, but they're all so *big*.

"Shit, it's the same here," Clothilde says, pointing to our left as we approach the Purpan hospital five minutes later.

Where there used to be an enormous cartridge factory… apartment buildings. Even bigger than the ones at Ponts Jumeaux and so many I can't even count them.

"Guess the city has grown since we saw it last," I say faintly.

We've seen the world evolving from our cemetery, of course. The cars in the parking lot have changed shapes, becoming less and less boxy and both larger and smaller, depending on the demographic driving them. Clothing has changed rather dramatically—several times—some outfits making both me and Clothilde stare in disbelief, some making us laugh ourselves silly, and some that have made even a deceased police officer who thought he'd seen it all feel very ill at ease.

I guess the biggest change we've seen remains the phones. One day, maybe in the late nineties, a man in a business suit came strolling into the cemetery with a bouquet of red roses for his deceased wife in one hand and a cordless phone in the other. He was talking into it, seemingly getting replies from the other end, so it appeared legitimate, though incredible. Today, everybody seems to have the things, and they can do the most wondrous things, from what I can gather.

As we drive through the streets of Toulouse, I see the phones everywhere; every other person seems to have their head bent with their nose to the small screens.

I haven't really spent a lot of time thinking about how the urban landscape can change over thirty years. The answer? Quite a lot.

Toulouse was already considered a big city when I was alive, but now it's…a bloody metropolis.

Sort of.

There don't seem to be any high-rise buildings anywhere. The tallest buildings we pass in the Saint Cyprien neighborhood were already there back in the day, and none of the new constructions seem to go past eight floors. So maybe big city would be a better description than metropolis.

Finally, we arrive at the hospital—also greatly changed since I last saw it but at the same time achingly familiar—and Evian and her young colleague await us in front of the morgue entry.

The second the back door opens, Clothilde and I both swoosh out. Clothilde moves away from us, clearly testing the limits of our bounds, but turns back after fifty meters or so.

"I *could* go farther if I had to," she tells me. "But it didn't feel very comfortable." A frisson goes through her, making her curls bounce around her head.

"No need to take any chances," I tell her. "We don't actually *want* to run away from these people, do we? They're the ones who can help us find your killer."

"Fair enough," Clothilde mumbles, but her gaze goes back to the place she turned back, a slight frown forming on her forehead.

Evian asks the people transferring the caskets from the hearse to the morgue to hurry up, frequently looking around, though I doubt anyone knows to care that she's bringing in two caskets instead of one.

As we finally enter the building, she seems to let out a long breath. "Welcome, friends," she says while patting Clothilde's casket. "Let's see what we can do to find you justice."

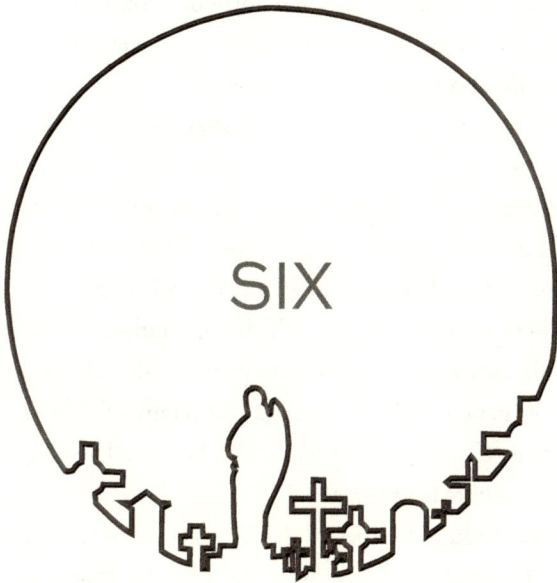

SIX

THEY PLACE OUR caskets side by side in an examination room. Looks like it was planned for only one casket but they manage to squeeze us both in. Evian has a word with the people who followed us in, probably making sure they won't talk to anyone about the second casket. She also negotiates the right for her and Malik to be the ones to open the caskets and without anyone else present.

I'm impressed she gets what she wants.

Then it's just Evian and her colleague left. And two ghosts, of course.

"I'm most curious about the tag-along," Evian says as she turns to grab what seems to be a tiny crowbar from the bench behind her. "But let's start with Mademoiselle Humbert." She fits the crowbar into a small crack in Clothilde's coffin and pulls until the wood creaks. She moves the crowbar ten centimeters farther down the lid and repeats the maneuver.

"Feel free to help, Malik," she says to her colleague, one eyebrow arched.

Malik seems to shake himself out of some sort of trance. "Right. Sure." He leans over the bench filled with various tools and grabs a second crowbar. "I'll take the other side?"

In no time at all, they have the lid of Clothilde's casket loose.

While they work, we ghosts move to the side along an empty, white workbench. I'm standing, leaning against the bench, while Clothilde is of course sitting on it, with her feet dangling through the cabinet doors below her.

"What should I expect?" Malik asks as he puts aside his crowbar. His eyes roam the casket and I'd say it might be his first time seeing a body that's been dead for thirty years. He seems nervous but I'm sure he won't chicken out.

Evian places her hands on the casket lid but takes the time to meet Malik's gaze and answer instead of just throwing it open like I'm sure she wants to. "It's a body that's been dead for thirty years, Malik. It's not going to pretty, but nor should she be recognizable. I'm guessing a skeleton with clothes."

"Gross," Clothilde says. Her eyes are intent on the casket and her attempt at humor is half-hearted at best.

"You don't need to look," I tell her. I know my turn is coming up, but right now I'm focused on my friend and I'm not sure what seeing her own decayed body will do to her. Unlike me, she wouldn't have seen a lot of dead people before she got killed—and only their ghosts in the thirty years since.

"Oh, I'm looking," she replies, but there's less bite in her tone than normal.

The two police officers grab hold of the casket's lid and lift it up on three. They carry it to the opposite wall and drop it gently in a corner.

"Oh, the horror!" Clothilde exclaims, now leaning over her casket to see what's inside.

I rush up next to her and look inside, expecting a gaping skull with empty eye sockets and lots of worms.

A mummified corpse lies there serenely, skin dark and tight over the skull, but the eyelids are still present, as are the lips, and the hair is most definitely Clothilde's, only with less shine and bounce.

She's in the traditional burial pose, with her hands crossed on her abdomen. The dress, a demure light yellow affair that covers her arms and legs all the way down to the ankles, is intact and could probably be reused if we found anyone who didn't mind a little grave robbing.

I'd have thought Clothilde had a sturdier stomach, but I guess seeing her own mummified body is a little much.

"That dress!" she exclaims, pointing at the yellow fabric. "Why would they bury me in *that*? My mom bought that when I was eighteen and we had the *worst* fight over it. It's *horrid* and *ugly* and…awful! I told her over my dead body—"

Her eyes widen and her hands clench at her side. "Ooooh! *Really?!?*"

"Horrid dress," Evian says as she bends over the casket.

The comment makes Clothilde deflate a fraction, enough to make her stop screaming. "*Thank you*," she says to Evian.

Malik makes a sound that makes me think his first reaction was to laugh but tried to keep it back.

Evian looks up at him, assessing him with a glint in her eyes. "No, it's probably not relevant to our case. But look at that thing." She waves a hand over Clothilde's corpse. "No young girl in her right mind would want to spend eternity dressed like that. Not even in the eighties."

Clothilde groans and pulls at her hair with both hands. "I've been wearing that monstrosity for thirty years, Robert. *Thirty years!* How *could* she? I'd kill her if she wasn't dead already."

"I thought it was your uncle who organized your funeral?" I say while keeping my eyes on Evian's assessment of the casket. At the moment, she's touching nothing but makes a slow circuit around the body, taking everything in.

"And he would have asked my mom for a dress. And she chose *that*."

I shrug. "You can yell at her once we figure out what happened to you and you join her on the other side."

Clothilde snorts at that idea but she seems to have calmed down. She steps back to let Evian past and we both go silent as the captain starts talking to her colleague.

"She was probably embalmed," Evian explains. "The casket is high quality but still wood and it was placed in dirt, not a cement chamber like it's done in some places. It means most of the body tissue has rotted away but some parts, like the skin, have mummified. Hair can hold for a surprisingly long time."

Malik nods along at her explanations and bends down to peer closer at Clothilde's hands and her head and hair. He holds his hands behind his back, probably to make sure he doesn't touch anything rather than a natural tendency toward parade rest.

Evian slips a phone out of an inner pocket of her jacket and starts taking pictures of the dead body.

I've seen this a couple of times in the cemetery. The phones are replacing cameras. And from what I've been able to see over our visitors' shoulders, the quality is surprisingly good. Still, this can't have taken the place of the painstakingly detailed photos that coroners used to take in my time?

"The coroner will take lots of official photos," she explains to Malik, making me wonder if I'd voiced my question. "But I like to make some of my own, in case I need to remember some detail while on a scene elsewhere."

She puts her phone back in her pocket and picks up the crowbar again. "Shall we have a look at our Monsieur X?"

SEVEN

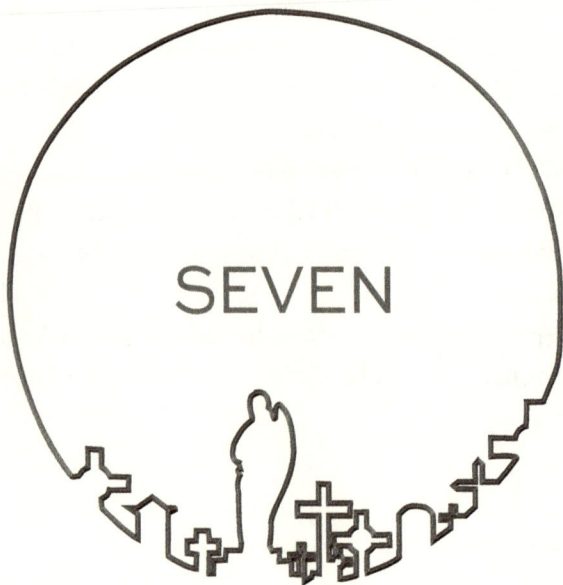

I HAD NO qualms about seeing Clothilde's dead body, but now that it is my turn, it feels like I have a stomach again, and it's filled with butterflies. I have no idea what to expect—or, actually, I do. But the decayed bodies I saw when I was a police officer all belonged to other people. This is *my* body. Or whatever is left of it.

Malik and Evian stand on opposite sides of the casket, crowbars poised. On Evian's nod, they both push down.

A small creak, a slight pop, and the sound of tumbling wooden planks and the entire casket disintegrates.

It seems like the lid was essential for the continued solidity of my casket and once the nails pulled free, all four sides fell outward and to the floor.

Evian must have expected it—or she has lightning quick reflexes—because she catches the lid before it smashes into whatever it has been protecting for the last thirty years, and pushes it to the floor with the rest of the casket.

A skeleton. Some dirt. And something that might have been hair.

That's all that's left of my body.

"Has this one been dead longer?" Malik asks Evian.

I'm suddenly afraid that Evian will think her colleague is right. She'll think my body has been in the ground for a lot longer and will send me back to the cemetery without trying to figure out who I am and why I was in an unmarked grave.

I don't want to be sent back.

Evian shakes her head. "I can't guarantee anything and will let the coroner do his job, but I'm guessing this body was buried pretty much at the same time as the other one." She waves a hand to encompass the scattered remains of my casket. "He was buried in what was basically a wooden box, which has been buried in dirt for a long time. It's a wonder the box has held as well as it has. He probably wasn't embalmed so the body will have decomposed pretty quickly."

Malik keeps his hands behind his back, his knuckles white from clenching his fists, as he stares at his boss with a frown marring his forehead. "He?"

Evian's brows draw together quickly. She looks at the skeleton's pelvis. "Well," she says slowly. "I think it *is* a man—though I'll let the coroner confirm that, too, as I'm by no means an expert—but…" She trails off, her frown deepening.

It wasn't a slip of the tongue. She made an assumption. Without looking for the information when she first saw the skeleton, she assumed it was that of a male. If I'm reading her correctly, I'm even willing to bet she made the assumption before seeing the body/skeleton.

A professional like Evian shouldn't make assumptions like that.

Could my presence here have influenced her somehow? As ghosts, we have very little influence over the living, but it is possible. However, the only times I've made a difference in the living world is when I've worked for it actively. Like in the cemetery earlier, when I talked in the gravediggers' ears to get them to think it was no big deal to have found an extra casket and body.

I haven't tried to influence Evian in any way.

And yet, she knew the dead body belongs to a man.

Evian shakes out of it and straightens so she's standing at parade rest right next to the skull—my skull. She casts an assessing glance at Malik, probably to figure out if he'll tell anybody that she'd made an assumption based on instinct instead of fact.

I'm guessing he won't. He probably hasn't really realized that it *is* a mistake on her part.

And there lies the problem, if Evian wants to continue training and working with him.

"I made an assumption that it was male, Malik," she says and my respect for her raises another notch. "Which I shouldn't have. You should always listen to gut feelings when you have them, but never assume they're right until you have proof. Ignoring or foregoing facts, proof, or science is sure to lead you down the wrong path and to incorrect conclusions."

Malik's eyes widen in surprise as he realizes his boss is admitting to making a mistake but he's also taking in what she's saying. The boy has great potential.

"Still." Evian is looking at the parts of the skeleton that will reveal the sex of the deceased. "I think my assumption was right—but I have no idea why I formed such an assumption."

She heaves a frustrated sigh. "I'm guessing it would greatly help the case if I do figure that out." She shakes her head.

I know why, of course. But I don't think whispering in her ear that she made the assumption because she's in the company of both dead bodies' ghosts will go over all that well. She'll just have to keep wondering.

Malik hesitates for a moment before speaking up again. "Did this one not have clothes on?"

Evian frowns and looks down at the skeleton again and so do I. Clothilde is apparently reminded of her own clothing and stares daggers at the yellow dress her mummified body is covered in.

Since the conditions were so different, it wouldn't be surprising if my clothes had also rotted away. But usually there would be some trace of it somewhere. Right now I see nothing resembling any type of cloth.

Evian leans in, walks around to study the body from all sides, and looks back and forth between the naked skeleton and the clothed mummified body several times.

"I'm tempted to say he was buried without clothing," she says, a hint of surprise in her tone. "Good observation, Doubira."

Malik's chest puffs out with pride and he smiles at the praise.

"But." Evian raises a finger and an eyebrow. "Also to be confirmed by the experts."

"Of course, Madame."

"On that note…" Evian uses her phone to take more pictures before moving toward the exit. "We're going to let the coroner do his job and come back once he's done."

Two minutes later, they're out the door.

I make a half-hearted effort to follow them, but the minute the door closes, I'm sucked back to the room where my skeleton lies, effectively closed off from the outside world.

"You've been naked for thirty years," Clothilde says with a shit-eating grin. Then she frowns and puts her hands on her hips. "Why were you buried naked?"

I shrug, but I'm secretly happy ghosts aren't stuck with wearing the clothes they were buried in. "Beats me. But I'm guessing finding out will get us one step closer to finding my killer."

EIGHT

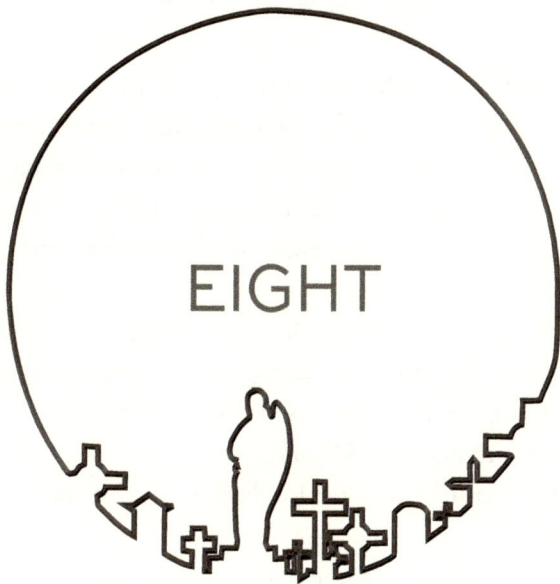

EMELINE STANDS ON her brand new balcony, admiring the view. She's on the Place Jeanne d'Arc, which is primarily occupied by a major bus hub on her left. Straight ahead, the statue of Joan of Arc stands proudly on her bronze horse, and in front of her, the rue d'Alsace Lorraine runs a straight line through the city center.

It's bound to be noisy, with the traffic from the boulevard, the buses coming and going at all hours, and the music from the merry-go-round at the beginning of Alsace Lorraine, but Emeline doesn't mind. She's from Paris, after all, where her apartment is in a place at least as noisy as this.

The balcony is small. She *might* be able to fit a small table and two chairs out here, not that she'll even try. She enjoys just standing here, leaning on the balcony and observing the people going past on the street below her, unaware that they're being watched.

The real estate agent had been surprised when Emeline said she'd take the apartment five minutes after seeing it. Emeline doesn't care. She wants a place with a bedroom, a living room, a kitchen, and a bathroom. Someplace safe and not too far from the police station. Somewhere central. The fact that it offers such a charming view is a bonus.

She'll call her contact at the police station in a minute to confirm with them that she's taking the first listing they offered her. Perhaps it can even count as something in her favor, to prove that she isn't trying to be difficult.

If she's causing difficulties for them at work, it's because she's doing her job.

Which is trying to figure out if some of their officers were doing a piss-poor job on purpose or if they're just incompetent— so she's bound to make a few people unhappy.

Ah, well.

She's starting to feel the cold of the April evening, so she returns inside the apartment and shuts the balcony door behind her. She can still hear the hum of the cars outside but it's not too bad. Her bedroom is on the other side, the window giving onto a tiny courtyard, so she shouldn't have any trouble sleeping at night.

Not because of the noise, anyway.

The place comes furnished. The living room has a small flat-screen TV, a scratched coffee table, and a surprisingly comfortable two-seater couch. The kitchen is open, with two high chairs pushed up against the counter, a small fridge, and an electric kettle that's going to see some use.

The bedroom has a queen-sized bed and a built-in closet, which is everything she'll need in there. The bathroom unfortunately doesn't have a bathtub but the shower seems clean and comfortable.

This place will do just fine.

She retrieves the keys from where the real estate agent left them on her way out and stifles a yawn. The thought of a shower and a bed has her eyes watering. She'll make the short walk to the hotel she's been staying at until now, get her things and check out, and come back here to crash early.

She has big plans for tomorrow.

Clothilde and Monsieur X—she *knows* he was a man but *cannot* figure out why she made that assumption—have secrets to tell her and she needs to be well rested so she doesn't miss anything.

As she's locking her door on her way out, the neighboring door flies open with such force that Emeline can feel the air being sucked toward the door as it swings inward.

A tiny woman appears and practically jumps out the door and slams it shut behind her. Her key is halfway to the keyhole when she sees Emeline standing there and freezes.

The woman's not exactly short, but far from tall. Her nose reaches Emeline's jaw. The nose in question is soft and a little wide and is framed by two startlingly large and clear green eyes. Her black hair is a glorious tangle of curls reaching not quite halfway down her neck.

"Oh!" she exclaims when she spots Emeline, in a voice too loud for such a small and empty space. "I didn't see you there. I hope I didn't scare you." She glances from the keys still in Emeline's hand to the door to Emeline's new apartment. "Are you moving in? I haven't seen you around here before."

"Yes, I just got the keys," Emeline says, jangling the keys before shoving them in the front pocket of her jacket. "Not sure how long I'll be staying, though."

"Oh, don't you worry about this place. It's great. The neighbors are either nice or basically invisible, the noise level is never a problem—except when the neighborhood cats decide to have a fight in the courtyard but it doesn't happen too often—and you can get anywhere on foot. You know the metro's right around the corner, right?"

The keys in her hand make a noise when she points in the direction of the metro, and it seems to remind her of what she was doing before the verbal diarrhea started. She shoves one of the keys in the lock and turns it quickly.

"You on your way out?" she asks with a huge smile that shows off a line of perfectly white teeth. "I kind of have to run or I'll be late for work." She starts walking down the hallway.

Emeline figures she might as well keep the woman company and so she follows her down the hallway and down the two flights of stairs. The other woman might have shorter legs but she practices something between a skip and a run and Emeline has to hurry to keep up.

"I'm Amina, by the way. I've lived here for three years now. And I'm always late so I don't think I've ever not run down these stairs. Are you from Toulouse?"

She pauses long enough for Emeline to answer. "No, I'm from Paris. I'm here for work."

Amina stops on the second-to-last step and turns to face Emeline. "A *Parisienne*?" She breathes a theatrical sigh. "Ah, well, I'll try not to hold it against you."

Emeline smiles. "How magnanimous of you."

"Yes, I know." Amina flashes that gleaming smile again, and then she's off toward the building's front door. "Anyway, I really gotta run. I hope we'll get the chance to get to know each other better sometime!"

Emeline waves a goodbye and watches as Amina runs down the sidewalk and disappears around the corner in the direction of the metro.

Making new friends wasn't part of the plan for her stay in Toulouse. But now the opportunity has presented itself, she realizes it's exactly what she'll need if the job takes as long as she's starting to think it will. She can't spend all her time thinking of nothing but work—that way lies madness.

A smiling and talkative neighbor might be exactly what she needs.

NINE

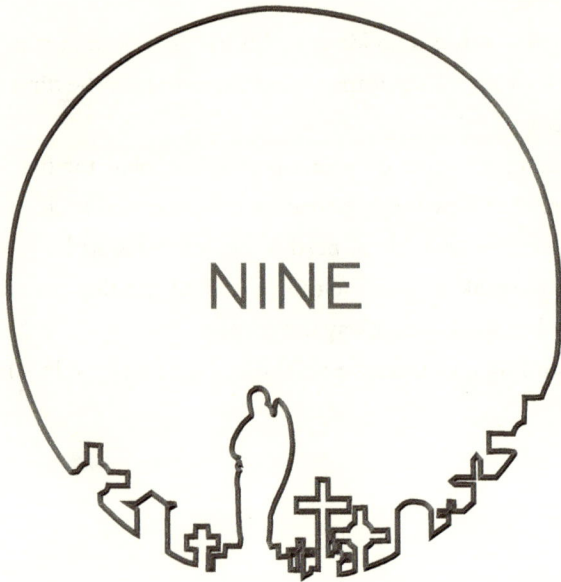

BEING STUCK IN a cemetery for thirty years can get very boring. At first, you panic at being dead and a ghost, and go through all the stages of grief. Then you try everything you can to get out of the cemetery, only to discover that the other ghost is right, there is no way out. Then you explore the cemetery itself, partly looking for clues on how to get out, partly trying to keep yourself occupied.

Well, the cemetery had nothing on this room in the city morgue. I am *bored*. Out of my mind.

And it's only been a night.

I'm torn between hoping we'll be kept here for a long time so we'll have more time to participate in the investigation into our own deaths, and hoping we'll be sent home to our graves very quickly so that we won't be going in circles in here for too long.

"We should try to tell the coroner to bring some books or something," Clothilde says from her perch on one of the cabinets. She started out on the bench but as she got increasingly bored, she moved to a higher seating arrangement. "This place should have better amenities for ghosts. I'm sure we're not the first ones to come through."

True enough. I'm lying on air next to my own skeleton, pretending there's a table here, staring into my own empty eye sockets, looking for answers.

Seriously, staying here for too long will not be good for my sanity.

"Be my guest," I tell Clothilde, waving at the man standing over her dead body, scalpel in hand.

Clothilde grunts in reply.

The man was here all yesterday afternoon and evening and came in quite early this morning. He's working hard—but has no affinity for ghosts *at all*. We've tried talking to him and touching him, telling him to talk to himself while he works, or make notes in a place that we can see, so that we can learn what he learns, but to no avail. The man is impossible to influence.

So we've given up on accompanying him while he works and we're now trying to find other ways to pass the time.

So far, we're not very successful.

At nine o'clock sharp, Captain Evian and Lieutenant Doubira return.

I jump up from my morbid slumber and Clothilde glides down from the cabinets to stand next to me. "Finally!" she says with feeling. "You wouldn't believe how much I missed you guys."

Evian smiles and looks to the side—right at us. Except she sees through us, of course, then frowns, and turns to face the coroner.

"In the same way that he's totally shut off," I say, pointing at the coroner, "I think she's rather open to communication. That's not the first time she's reacted when we talk, and we're not even standing particularly close."

Clothilde walks over to stand behind Evian, goes up on tiptoe, and blows on the captain's neck.

Evian shivers and runs a hand over her neck, like she is swatting away a mosquito.

Clothilde returns to stand next to me with a big grin. "I do believe you're right. Could be useful!"

I fold my arms over my chest and try not to let the hope take too much of a hold. "Unless we're sent back to the cemetery never to see her again."

Clothilde slaps the back of my head. I can't feel it but still throw her an annoyed glance.

"Positive energy, Robert," she says. "Otherwise there's no hope for us, be it here or in the cemetery."

I push the mental chatter away and focus on Evian, who is shaking hands with the coroner and settles next to the empty workbench along the wall, at parade rest as always.

"I got your message this morning," she says. "You already have a preliminary report?"

"Yes," the coroner says. "I will need a couple more days before my analysis is complete, but I believe I have some elements that may help you continue your investigation."

"I appreciate that," Evian says, genuine sincerity in her voice.

The coroner points to my skeleton. "Monsieur X is indeed male. He was probably in his mid-thirties when he died,

44

which was about thirty years ago. I'd say within a year or so of Mademoiselle Humbert's death."

I exchange a glance with Clothilde. So far, he's got everything right.

"He was 1.82 meters, was Caucasian, white, brown hair. Broke his leg at some point but it's probably irrelevant because it happened while he was a teenager."

My eyebrows rise. I'm impressed. "Skiing accident," I explain to Clothilde.

"Shoulders have both been displaced at least once, and he's had a broken middle finger on the right hand and a broken nose."

I touch my nose in memory. "Nose was from a stupid bar fight while I was a student, but the rest were in the line of duty."

Evian speaks up. "Sounds like he's had a rather eventful life."

The coroner casts a quick glance at my skeleton. "I'd say an athlete or someone with a physically dangerous job."

Clothilde moves closer to Evian, her eyes intent. When the coroner makes his remark, she leans in to whisper in Evian's ear, "He was a police officer."

"Like a police officer," Evian says immediately.

The coroner stops talking, his mouth still open, and Malik turns in surprise. Clothilde sends me a thumbs-up.

The slightest hint of color appears on Evian's cheeks—she's embarrassed she interrupted the other man, and with another assumption, no less.

"Or a firefighter," she adds belatedly. "Or any kind of construction work, really."

"All of those theories would be valid," the coroner says. He pauses for a moment, waiting to see if Evian has anything else to add. When she stays quiet, he continues his report.

"He probably died of a gunshot."

Clothilde's eyes find mine and I see the question in them. I never knew how I'd been killed. I don't even know for sure that I was killed, I've just always assumed. But I could have died of natural causes, for all I knew. Now this guy can tell simply from looking at my skeleton that I was shot?

"How do you know?" Evian asks. Her question is polite, in no way insinuating that the coroner could be wrong, but like me, she must think it to be a bit of a long shot.

The coroner points to a spot on my skeleton's torso. "The bullet's still there."

"What?" Clothilde yells. "How did we not see that? You've been staring at that thing for almost twenty hours."

"In my defense, it was dark for at least eight of those," I say, but my voice is weak. I lean over to look at the spot the man is pointing at and now that I know what I'm looking for, I spot the bullet.

It's as black as the dirt on the table and it's lodged in the juncture between my spine and my fifth rib. If I was shot from the front, the bullet probably went through the heart before stopping there.

"Well, that's one question answered," Clothilde murmurs.

I move away as Evian comes closer to observe the same thing I did. "Shot through the heart?" she asks and I shiver at the echo of my own thought.

"If the person shooting was a little taller than him and shooting from shoulder height, yes," the coroner answers. When no other questions ensue, he continues his report. "I'll need to run a more thorough analysis but so far I see no proof of any clothing. It appears he was buried naked."

"Looks like I'll be going through old missing persons' reports," Evian says as she straightens and resumes parade rest. "If he was shot, then buried naked in an unmarked grave, I think we can assume the burial wasn't done by anybody who cared about him."

On a certain level, I already knew this—after all, nobody bothered with a headstone and I've never had a single visitor—but it still shakes me. Did my family search for me when I disappeared? Did my friends? My colleagues?

Did my disappearance cause pain to people I care about? Or did it hardly make an impact because nobody cared?

It bothers me that I don't have answers to those questions.

The coroner puts a hand on my skull—the one belonging to the skeleton on the table, not ghost me—in what I think is affection. "That's all I have on Monsieur X at the moment."

Evian nods, clearly curious about who I was and how I ended up on this table, but accepting that she'll have to wait for the rest.

"Now, to Mademoiselle Humbert," the coroner says and moves to stand next to her body. "Clothilde." Somehow, since he's been impervious to our attempts at communication, I've assumed he's not empathetic. The catch in his voice as he says Clothilde's name says otherwise.

"Clothilde had a rough time of it," he says. "First of all, she was raped before she died."

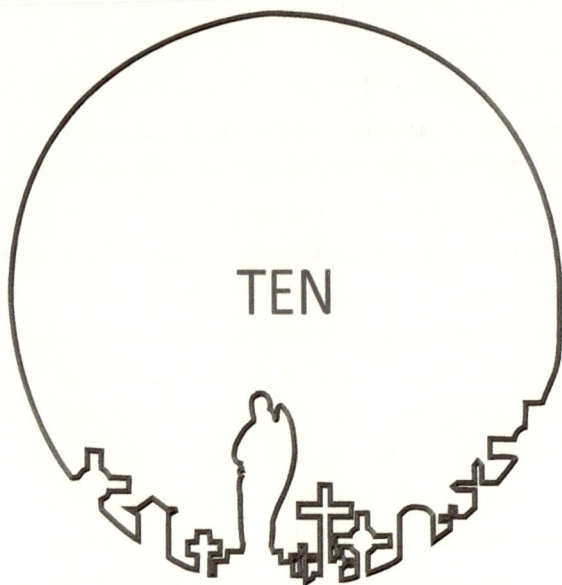

TEN

CLOTHILDE'S JAW JUTS out and she folds her arms over her chest when the coroner makes his statement. She stands right next to Evian, staring across her own mummified body at the man who claims she'd been raped before she was killed. Malik has taken up position next to the coroner.

We had our suspicions about the rape, honestly. After all, the reason we are here right now is that two young girls came through our cemetery as ghosts and while investigating their murders, we discovered that they appeared to have been killed by the same people who killed Clothilde. The two girls had been raped, so it stood to reason that Clothilde might have, too.

Still, getting the confirmation can't feel good.

Clothilde's eyes roam her own corpse. "I thought they cleaned bodies before funerals."

I look to the coroner to see if he picks up on Clothilde's remark, but of course he doesn't.

"You found DNA? Or were there torn tissues?" With Evian, it's difficult to tell if she picks up on our conversation or if she's just doing good police work. I'm tempted to say it's a little bit of both.

"DNA," the coroner answers and my non-existent heart rate doubles.

Could it really be that simple? A sample of DNA and we find Clothilde's killer after all these years?

Will she move on so soon?

The coroner doesn't leave me time to ponder. "The body was cleaned and embalmed before burial but they mostly focus on the exterior. I found a relatively large sample of semen. We'll have a DNA profile quite soon."

Malik seems to be holding his breath as he stares wide-eyed at his superior. "Do you think we'll find a match? On a thirty-year-old death?"

"Thirty-year-old murder," Clothilde and Evian say in unison.

Clothilde turns to study Evian's profile with a satisfied half-smile on her lips and Evian shivers and runs a hand over her neck.

"I want you to run that DNA against a specific profile," Evian says to the coroner.

The man's eyebrows shoot up. "You have a suspect on a case this old?"

Evian nods but her eyes are distant as she looks at the mummified corpse on the table in front of her. "A sixty-year-old police officer who will soon be on trial for six recent rapes and murders."

"Six," the coroner repeats.

"Probably more, but we only have DNA evidence for those six," Evian says. Her gaze comes back into focus and she fixes the other man with a firm glare. "No talking to anyone about this."

The coroner lifts his chin. "I would never." He's offended by Evian's assumption that he'd talk about confidential information outside of work. Good.

"Do you have any way of knowing if she had any medication or poisoning in her system when she died?" Malik asks his first question without conferring with Evian and it's a good one.

I nod at the young man in approval even though he can't see it, and I see the gesture mirrored on Evian.

The coroner shoves his hands into the pockets of his white lab coat. "I've managed to get some samples from the better preserved parts, so it's possible. The samples are on their way to the laboratory as we speak. I should have some preliminary results by the end of the day."

He looks between the two police officers. "You have reason to believe she was poisoned?"

Evian's gaze is focused on Clothilde's sunken face. "All the others were."

Silence settles as all three alive persons in the room stare at Clothilde's corpse. I prefer to stare at the real Clothilde—the ghost—trying to figure out how she's feeling about all this.

"You think it's the same guy who killed Manon and Lise?" I ask her.

"It's the same guy who did the rape," Clothilde answers. She's keeping her eyes on Evian, studying her closely, looking for…something. "I don't know who did the actual killing. The poisoning was done by Laurent Lambert. He's still at large."

50

Laurent Lambert. The lawyer with a name so generic it doesn't even feel real. The man who we know poisoned Lise and who had a meeting with Manon on the day she died and remembered nothing about.

The man who rented the hotel room that Clothilde died in.

"It would still be helpful to know if he was the one to rape you," I say softly. "Everybody will know this has been going on for a long time."

Clothilde nods, her eyes still on Evian.

"Maybe it will help you to move on," I say.

Clothilde finally tears her eyes away from Evian and meets my gaze. "We already knew I was killed by the same people as Lise and Manon. We suspected I'd been raped. Catching the rapist was enough for them to move on but for me it's not. Laurent Lambert needs to pay."

The anger in her midnight voice makes me take a step back. Her eyes are black and her curly hair moves around her head like there's a wind playing with it. There's a calm about her that makes all my cop's reflexes go on high alert.

I know she has carried around a lot of anger since her death but I've often put a lot of it down to her being stuck as a moody teenager.

I'm starting to realize just how angry she is. And that it's *justified*.

Keeping eye contact, I nod. "He *will* pay, Clothilde. We'll make sure of it." I nod in the direction of Evian. "*She'll* make sure of it."

Clothilde stares at Evian again, to the point where the captain throws a nervous glance around the room—that woman is *very* attuned to otherworldly activities—and finally nods, mostly to herself, I think.

51

"She seems good," Clothilde says. "She seems good, right?"

"She does," I agree.

"Good." She lets out a frustrated sigh and I relax slightly now that the midnight voice is gone. "God, I wish I could come with her during the investigation."

"You and me both," I tell her. "I'm guessing we have another day here, max, before we're sent back to the cemetery."

"I don't want to go back." She juts out her jaw and frowns down at her own dead body as if it has done her a great injustice. Which, to be fair, it sort of has.

She slides closer to Evian and leans in to whisper straight into her ear. "You should take the bodies with you during your investigation. I'm sure they'd be really helpful."

I can tell that Evian is bothered because she does a whole-body shiver so I do my best to keep my laughter in. That wouldn't help her understand what she's feeling at all. I can just picture it, the investigator dragging two corpses around everywhere she goes, arguing that it will help her solve the case.

"We need to come with you," Clothilde continues in her creepy whisper. "We can help you solve the case. We're so bored in that cemetery."

Evian shakes her shoulder, clearly trying to shake Clothilde off even though she doesn't realize it. "All right, Doubira, I think we've seen enough here for today."

Doubira's eyebrows shoot up in surprise but to his credit, he doesn't say anything.

"You'll send me the complete report when you're done?" Evian asks the coroner. "What you've told us so far has been very helpful."

"Uh…" The man seems to have trouble following the sudden change in mood in Evian, which is understandable, especially for someone who wouldn't have caught *any* of the otherworldly conversations in the room. "Of course. I'll make sure it's in your inbox by the end of the day."

"Thank you." And without another word, Evian almost runs out the door, with Doubira scurrying out after her.

I wait a few seconds before speaking. "That wasn't very nice, Clothilde. You scared the captain."

Clothilde shrugs and jumps up to perch on the empty workbench along the wall. "She can take it." She looks longingly at the door where Evian and Doubira disappeared. "Imagine what we could do if we could assist her during the investigation. She's *so* receptive."

"I know," I reply.

But that's never going to happen.

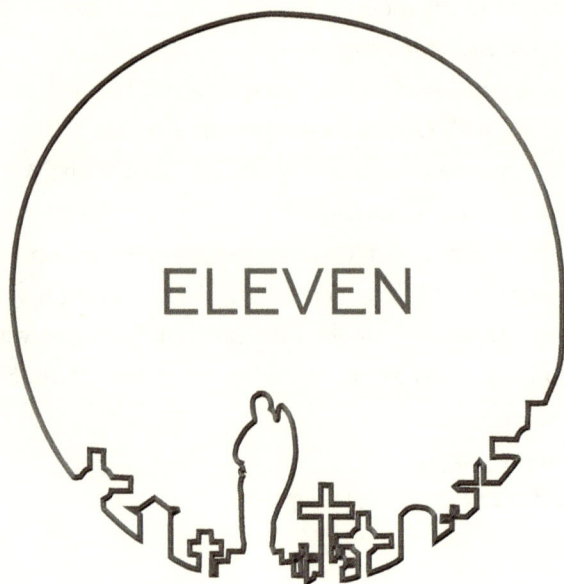

ELEVEN

THE CORONER CONTINUES working for a couple of hours, still not talking to himself, so we don't know if he finds anything interesting. Before leaving, he stands next to Clothilde's body and puts his hand on hers—or what remains of them, anyway, mere bones barely covered with a thin, dry skin—apparently saying goodbye. But without saying anything out loud, of course.

"Seems like you made an impression," I say.

"You jealous?" Clothilde is on her workbench perch, Converse-clad feet dangling through the cupboard and hands under her thighs. She's back to her usual self, the anger nowhere in sight.

I know it's lurking not far beneath the surface.

I grin at her. "I'd be more affected by the young girl who was raped and murdered than the middle-aged man who'd clearly led a rough life, too."

She shrugs. "We'll both go back to the cemetery, anyway."

With a slight squeeze, the coroner finishes his goodbyes and exits the room, leaving just the two of us.

Four of us?

I'm going to go with two. That skeleton hasn't been me for a very long time, and I don't think Clothilde identifies much with the mummified thing either.

Speaking of which…as I watch the folded hands of Clothilde's corpse, they move.

"What the…" I move closer, peering at the fingers. They don't seem quite as solid as they were earlier. Could the coroner touching them have made what remained of the skin fall apart?

Another movement. Now that I'm staring at it, I can see it's the little finger of her right hand that's falling away from the rest of the hand. It's still attached—sort of—by a piece of skin so thin I can see right through it.

"What's so interesting?" Clothilde asks.

I wave for her to approach. "Come over here, will you? Look." I point at the finger. "I think your finger's coming off."

She rolls her eyes, proving that teenager Clothilde is indeed back. "Gross."

I eye the cloth of her yellow dress, which goes all the way to the end of the table. "Would you mind trying to get it to fall off all the way?"

"What?"

I've surprised her. It's good to know it's still possible. "You're better than me at affecting the living world—"

"I wouldn't really call this 'living.'"

55

"—and I'm wondering what would happen if your finger stays behind here."

Clothilde catches my meaning immediately. She eyes the barely attached finger, the cloth leading the way to the edge of the table, and the floor. "You think I could stay with the finger if they leave it behind?"

I meet her gray eyes and lift one shoulder. "Won't know unless we try, will we?"

We're clearly linked to our dead bodies. Wherever the bodies are stuck, so are we.

But what happens if the body is in several pieces? Can we choose which part to follow?

It's certainly worth a try.

So Clothilde does her thing, rushing around like an angry poltergeist, throwing herself at the finger. I step away in order to avoid being in her way and not getting too dizzy with all the movement, and I admire her work. For a ghost, she certainly has a lot of energy.

It takes over an hour, but it works.

The last strip of skin lets go and the bones of the little finger fall off the hand. They tumble down along the folds of the yellow dress and tumble off the table and to the floor.

Three small bones clatter to the floor, the sound like sticks knocking together.

Clothilde shivers and shakes out her right hand. "Gha...that felt weird."

We both stare at the bones on the floor. They're very visible, at least the first two, so chances are that someone will pick them up and put them back on the dead body shortly. Still, it was worth a shot.

"Want me to try on yours?" Clothilde asks.

I look at my skeleton and shake my head. "We won't be able to make any bone move that far." My bones are all lying flat, basically a 2D image instead of the 3D one that Clothilde's body presents, and there are no clothes to help us along.

"I can't just stay behind if you go back to the cemetery," Clothilde says. She's worried, and I'm not entirely certain if it's for me or for herself. We've been in each other's company for so long, neither of us is comfortable with the idea of splitting up.

"You can, and you will," I tell her sternly. "If you have a chance to figure out what happened thirty years ago, you have to take it. We'll never get anywhere working out of the cemetery."

She's not happy about it but I can tell she'll do it. She really does need to get out there to find her killer.

"If you miss me too much," I say, meaning if she gets stuck here in the morgue and it turns out even more boring than the cemetery, "your body will be in the cemetery with me. You can come back."

Clothilde's eyebrows draw together as she eyes the finger bones on the floor. "You think that'd work?"

I have no idea. How am I supposed to know? "Maybe?"

We both burst out laughing.

TWELVE

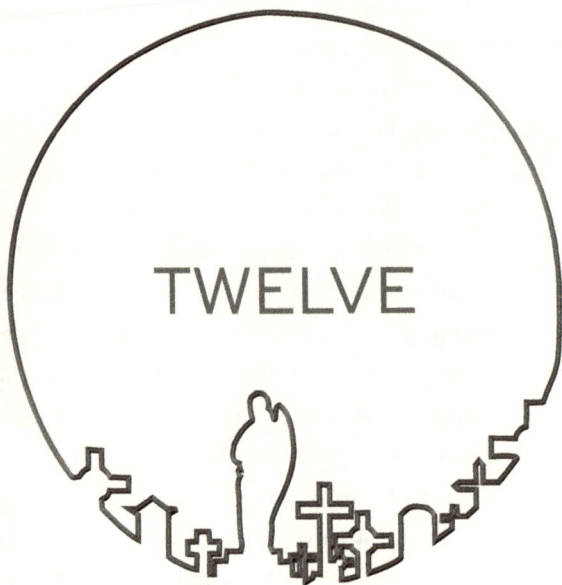

EMELINE WANTS TO be present when they send the bodies back to the cemetery. She feels like she owes them at least that much.

When she enters the examination room where the coroner did his job, there are already five other people present. They've brought back Clothilde's original casket and somebody has fixed up the little dents Emeline and Malik made in the lid when they forced it open.

For Monsieur X, they've brought a body bag. Until they figure out who this guy was, he's not going back to the cemetery. Emeline briefly played with the idea of shoving him into Clothilde's casket but quickly came to her senses.

She can't even understand why she had the urge to make sure the two aren't separated. Sure, they've been buried together for thirty years but they're *dead bodies*. Monsieur X is nothing but a heap of bones.

They don't care.

And yet, Emeline does.

She wants the two to stay together and she wants their bodies to be treated with respect. Which is why she's here to supervise the transport rather than getting a nice meal from the Chinese restaurant just around the corner from her new apartment and relaxing with a book.

There are too many people in here. Because of her request not to disturb the bodies, there are four technicians to lift Clothilde into her casket.

Emeline has an urge to walk to the other side of the room—so she does.

She has these weird feelings when working cases sometimes and she's learned not to fight them. Her subconscious thinks she might see something interesting from the other side of the room, so she'll go there to have a look.

Everything looks the same.

But what's that on the floor?

She takes a step closer, bending down to see between the legs of the woman closest to her.

Something has fallen to the floor close to the working table where Monsieur X's skeleton lies.

It's a finger. The three knuckles of a finger lie forgotten on the floor, close to being stepped on by the technicians.

Emeline takes two steps closer to Clothilde's casket to look at the mummified corpse that is now back to its final resting place.

The little finger of the right hand is missing.

Clothilde's little finger is on the floor.

Without thinking, Emeline bends down and picks up the three knuckles. She has the urge to put them in her pocket.

Why would she do that?

Still, the urge is strong. She stands there, in the way of the technicians who are moving to put the lid on the casket, with three bones in her hand, and although her mind is telling her to put the things into the casket with the rest of the body, her hand is moving toward her pocket.

Emeline's breathing becomes erratic and little stars appear at the edge of her vision like they do sometimes when her brain isn't getting enough oxygen. The ventilation system seems louder than the voices of the people around her, and the smells of antiseptic and dirt make her want to sneeze.

She sees a movement out of the corner of her eye, something that looks like a dark-haired girl, but when she turns to look, there's nothing there.

She takes a deep breath. Another one.

Tries to think.

It's another one of her gut reactions, nothing more. She's always had them and they have always served her well. Perhaps her subconscious wants her to keep a memento of the girl who was killed but never found justice, to make sure she doesn't give up on the case.

But it's *bones*.

"Wait," she says as the technicians lower the lid to Clothilde's casket. She steps forward and slips her hand through the gap between casket and lid and drops the bones inside. She nods, indicating they can close the lid.

Bloody hell, maybe she really should have gone with the book and Chinese option tonight. She wouldn't risk grave robbing.

As the technicians bring out the body bag that Monsieur X will live in until they figure out who he was and where he *should* be buried, Emeline takes a step back and puts her hands in her pockets.

Her right hand touches on something.

Her breath catches and her heart beats loudly in her ears as she slowly pulls the object out of her pocket.

A knuckle.

It's the smallest of the three bones she found on the floor, a tiny piece of mummified skin still stuck to the tip. Somehow, she managed to throw only two of three bones into the casket, and the third one found its way into her pocket instead, like her subconscious wanted.

Emeline sighs. Well, if her subconscious wants it that bad, it can have it. She's not asking the technicians to reopen the casket so she can admit to stealing a bone.

She takes three steps so she's standing between two of the technicians at Monsieur X's table. She grabs onto the cloth covering the table, like they have.

Now what?

It's like Emeline has lost all control of her body. First, she slips a bone into her own pocket without realizing it, and now she's butting in on somebody else's job for no apparent reason.

The technicians look at her sideways but don't say anything. They'll apparently let her "help" if that's what she wants.

Oh, look, more finger bones.

The thought pops into her head so loudly it's like someone is standing right next to her, yelling it into her ear.

And the voice is right. She's standing at the level of Monsieur X's left hand, where the bones cannot be recognized as a hand anymore but it's the right location and Emeline knows enough about the human body to recognize the little bones for what they are.

She has an overwhelming urge to steal one of them.

It wouldn't be stealing if the owner wants you to have it.

Now where did *that* thought come from?

Something very strange is going on here. She's tired and somewhat stressed out about this case, but not to the point of hallucinations and grave robbing. Something in this place makes her behave strangely—but in a way that has happened so many times in the past when she followed her gut feeling. A feeling that has yet to lead her in the wrong direction.

Her gut is telling her that she should have a piece of Monsieur X's skeleton.

"On three," the technician standing next to Emeline says.

Now or never. Emeline grabs the cloth with the others, making sure to grab close to the collection of fine bones from Monsieur X's hand.

On three, she lifts with the others, but also slips one of the bones into her hand. When Monsieur X is in the body bag, she drops the bone into the pocket where Clothilde's little finger is.

The elation she feels makes her want to jump from joy—which would be downright rude and weird considering the circumstances.

She needs to get out of here before she does something she'll regret, or something that will draw attention to her little theft.

"Thank you for letting me be present," she tells the technicians, all of whom regard her somewhat oddly—understandable, since she hasn't actually done anything but stand there and watch, as far as they know.

Then she hightails it out of the morgue, one hand in her pocket, playing with the bones.

For the first time since exhuming the bodies of Clothilde and Monsieur X, the feeling of being…not alone…doesn't go away as she leaves the bodies behind.

THIRTEEN

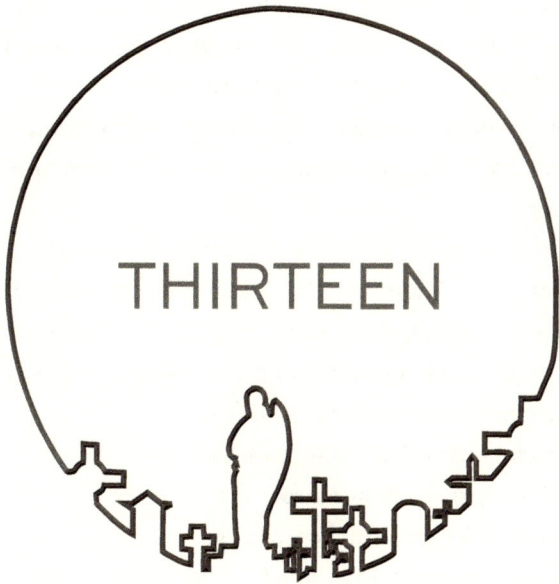

"WE MADE IT! We're out!" Clothilde jumps with a fist toward the sky like she just won the Olympics. Her hair is exuberant, her eyes shine, and her smile takes over her entire face. I think she's outshining the sun as it's beating down on us in front of the metallic doors of the morgue exit. I can almost feel the rays on my skin and I could swear I smell the lavender blossoms that line the path toward the parking lot.

I want to jump with joy like Clothilde but I'm also recovering from the fear of being abandoned all by myself in the morgue for who knows how long.

We both assumed our bodies would automatically be sent back to the cemetery. We had a faint hope that Clothilde could somehow remain behind because of the dislodged finger. But at no point did we envision the option where I'm left behind in a body bag in a morgue, where I'd have no say in how long I'd stay there and no way to help find my murderer.

I also wouldn't be able to help other ghosts move on, the only thing that has been keeping me sane as I work toward my own redemption.

While I froze in panic back there when I realized where my body was going, Clothilde didn't even hesitate. She yelled, she cajoled, she touched, she pushed. She did everything she could to get Evian to pick up a piece of my skeleton as well, so that I'd have the same chance as her at getting out.

Miracle worker that she is, it worked.

And to top it all off, our theory that we could follow the body part of our choice seems to be working.

It was far from a picnic, though. When Evian walked through the door of the morgue, I felt a slight pull at my left middle finger—the one that Evian had stolen the bone of—but it would clearly go away quickly if I ignored it.

When Evian passed the threshold, we both walked out with her, mentally grabbing onto the link we had with those tiny little bones, and forcing our way through the invisible barrier that the door represented for us.

It was like walking through mud, with weighted-down shoes. I felt my skeleton in that body bag pulling me back, stronger for every step I took past the threshold. Despite not having need for breath for over thirty years, I now took deep ones, searching for the strength needed to follow Evian wherever she was going with that little piece of me.

Clothilde struggled, too. She leaned forward as if she had a rope around her torso, pulling her backward. But she kept her eyes on the prize—Evian a few steps ahead of us—and kept fighting.

"Focus on the link to that finger," I told her, and forced myself to do the same. Instead of exerting myself thinking about the link to my body, the link I wanted to sever, I focused my energy on strengthening the link I wanted to keep.

I'm not saying it was easy, but it did the trick. When the door to the morgue slammed shut, we were on the far side of it, and I felt the link to my body snap like a released slingshot as I sped up to find myself as close to Evian's pocket as ghostly possible.

I didn't have to worry about Clothilde—she ended up in the exact same spot as me, making our ghostly forms overlap for a moment before we adapted to the new situation enough to take a step away from the tiny bones that were suddenly our only links to our dead bodies.

And now, here we are, outside the morgue and following the police officer who is trying to find our murderers.

Well, trying to find Clothilde's murderer and my identity, but same difference.

"I'm going to test the allowed distance," I tell Clothilde and stop walking.

Evian seems to be heading for the visitors' parking lot, which is less than one hundred meters away. I want to know how far away I can go when we're in a place with no obvious barriers.

"Do your thing, detective," she replies joyfully as she skips along next to Evian, grinning madly at the woman who is sensitive enough to otherworldly activities to have busted us out of that morgue. I do believe I'm seeing some hero worship, not that Clothilde would ever admit it.

I don't quite feel brave enough to walk away from Evian, but I stop where I am, letting her walk away from me.

Immediately, the need to run after her rises in my chest. I'm *really* not comfortable letting her walk away like that.

But I force myself to hold out. To feel the pull of my bond to that bone, how it pulls at my chest, at my entire being. When she's twenty meters away, I think I see filaments of my ghostly body escaping toward her, making me look more and more translucent as parts of me fly away.

When I realize it reminds me of how ghosts look when they're on the point of moving on to wherever ghosts who have found peace go, I get scared and run after Clothilde and Evian.

The moment I start moving closer to what remains of my dead body, I get back my filaments and become as solid as I've ever been in ghost form.

Not really in a state of mind to play too much with danger, I hurry to catch up with the two women.

"Well?" Clothilde asks me. She's walking backward, keeping an eye on Evian as she walks right through signposts and cars alike, not caring one whit about physical objects.

"Twenty meters became *very* uncomfortable," I tell her and shudder.

She nods. "I got farther on the day we arrived. Could the link be weaker because there's just the one bone now?"

A shiver runs through me as my left middle finger vibrates. I look to Evian and realize she has a hand in her pocket and must be touching the bones.

Clothilde's eyes go to the same place and she clenches her right fist. "It's weird actually feeling something."

I nod.

"That woman's crazy sensitive, by the way," Clothilde says. "We mention the bones and her hand goes straight to them."

"Maybe we should pay attention to what we say then," I say. "So we don't scare her off completely and make her get rid of the things. I don't feel like haunting a landfill for the rest of eternity."

Evian reaches her car—a white Peugeot 206 that is clearly a rental and has seen better days—and as she opens the door, Clothilde slips inside to settle into the passenger seat. She throws me a smile that is anything but reassuring.

Evian gets into the car and I hurry to follow. I'm not taking any chances right now. I settle into the back seat and lean forward between the seats to look Clothilde in the eyes as I talk to her. "Play nice," I tell her.

"I always play nice." She doesn't even try to pretend that's true.

Evian snorts as she turns the ignition.

FOURTEEN

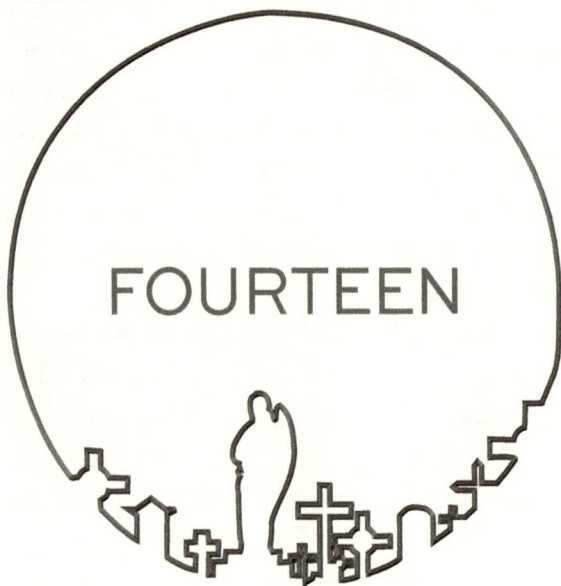

EVIAN BRINGS US straight to her apartment. She has a cozy one bedroom on Jeanne d'Arc, with a small but functional kitchen and a bedroom with plenty of closet space. At the moment, the closet is depressingly empty, with only enough clothes to fill one suitcase. It looks like she didn't plan to spend too much time in Toulouse and seeing how she's opening all the cupboards in search of a mug, I'm guessing she hasn't lived here long.

In an unspoken agreement, Clothilde and I leave her some space. We settle on the couch on the far side of the room and don't talk.

I'm not sure what I have to say, anyway.

68

I've been dreaming of getting out of that cemetery ever since I woke up screaming in my casket underground thirty years ago, but now that I'm out, I'm not sure what to do with myself.

The world has changed while I hustled around in my cemetery. I recognize the streets and the older buildings, the people are pretty much the same, and the noise of the city center is like it always was. But it's also so very different.

The clothes aren't quite right. The phones are everywhere. The cars are bigger, smaller, silent…different. The people are the same in general, but I don't recognize anyone. I'm in the city where I lived all my life, where I felt like I knew every other person on the street—and now I recognize nobody.

Nobody would recognize me if they saw me.

I'm starting to wonder, for the first time in a very long time, what my family and friends are up to. Do they still wonder what happened to me? Have they moved on?

Are they still alive?

I realize I'm overwhelmed. I'd say a good night's sleep will do me good, but ghosts don't need sleep. Ghosts *can't* sleep. Still, a night of nothing happening will probably help.

I just need to get my head on straight.

Then we can start again tomorrow, and take things one step at a time.

First things first: we'll be looking for Clothilde's murderer. The infamous Laurent Lambert.

My finger tingles and I look up to see Evian at her kitchen counter. She has removed her jacket and hung it on the back of the front door and she has a steaming cup of tea in her left hand.

With her right, she's playing with the two finger bones on the kitchen counter.

She's pushing them around like she's doing a puzzle and she can't figure out how the pieces fit together. Every time she touches my bone, my finger tingles.

From Clothilde's clenched fist, I'd say she feels the same thing.

"Who are you two, anyway?" Evian whispers.

Clothilde opens her mouth to answer, but I put a hand on her thigh to stop her. She can't feel it but seeing it is enough. Her eyes ask me why.

"Leave her some space to think for herself," I whisper.

Clothilde's gaze goes to Evian and she nods. She slides farther down into the couch, leaning her head against the headrest.

Evian takes a sip of her tea and winces at the heat. Her short dark blond hair stands out a little on one side of her head, where she must have run her hand through it as she brewed her tea. Other than that little detail, she's impeccably presentable in her black jeans, white shirt, and tiny golden necklace that I have yet to see the details of. After such a long and tiring day, this is no mean feat. The woman must be used to being in control of everything.

So being pushed into stealing two finger bones is probably messing with her head just a little bit.

"What the hell am I supposed to *do* with these?" she asks herself, making me wonder if it's possible for her to be so sensitive as to pick up on my *thoughts*.

She picks up the bones and stares at the trashcan in the corner. "I should just ditch them. I don't need the reminder of why I'm doing this." She walks over to the trashcan and pushes the pedal so it opens.

Clothilde jerks up next to me, but I hold up a hand to stop her from talking.

Evian needs to decide to keep us on her own.

And I do believe she does. She stands there, with her fist over the open trashcan, for what feels like hours. Her hand is clenched and I can see the muscles of her forearms working. It's like she's telling her hand to let go, but the hand's not obeying.

Finally, she lets the trashcan fall shut and her hand falls to her side while her chin drops to her chest. Then she raises her head, mutters, "Fuck it," and goes to drop the bones back into her jacket pocket.

I turn to smile at Clothilde. "I do believe we're in."

FIFTEEN

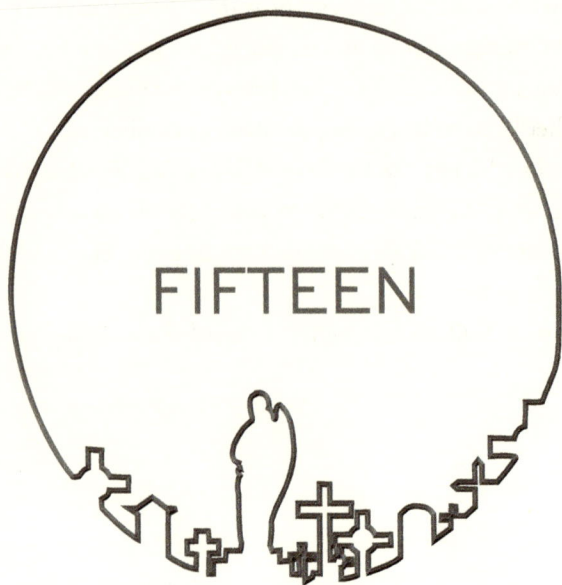

I'D SAY THE night is boring, with the two of us stuck in Evian's living room, but it's actually a lot more interesting than the cemetery we already know by heart. We study everything the place has—which isn't much other than the bare basics needed to get by—and settle on the couch to wait for morning to come.

We don't talk much. I think we both need some time to adapt to this new reality of ours and to let our thoughts settle. It seems like we may be allowed to tag along for the ride when Evian goes after Clothilde's murderers so it's important we keep our wits about us.

With someone as sensitive as Evian, I think we also need to watch what we say around her so as not to distract her from her work.

At seven o'clock the next morning, we hear an alarm clock going off in the bedroom, then the shower running. Ten minutes later, Evian comes through the door, wearing the same pants and a different shirt from yesterday, and her hair is wet but combed.

"Morning," she says as she enters the room.

Out of reflex, Clothilde and I both reply.

Evian stops in her tracks—just for a second—tilts her head, and scans the room. With a shake of her head, she sighs and resumes her walk toward the kitchen, where she immediately starts the water heater and prepares a mug of green tea.

As she waits for the water to boil, her gaze keeps going back to her jacket hanging on the back of the front door.

At our bones.

She leaves them where they are, though. She has a quick breakfast consisting of cereal with milk and an apple, makes a quick trip to the bathroom to brush her teeth and finish drying her hair, and by seven thirty she's putting on her comfortable-looking black running shoes and her jacket and walks out the door.

We're still sitting on the couch but the moment the door closes behind her, suddenly we're standing in the hallway, almost on top of her, as she locks the door.

"That's an efficient way of moving around," Clothilde comments lightly.

"Kind of confusing, though," I say, shaking my head. I might not have a physical form, but my mind is not used to going from one place to another in the blink of an eye without having told my ghostly form to go there.

We take a few steps away from Evian, to give her some space, then trail after her as she walks toward the staircase. I *could* continue testing our bond to her—or rather to those finger bones—but I don't feel like it today. Right now, being close to Evian is exactly where I want to be, anyway.

We run across a neighbor on the staircase, a beautiful woman with skin the color of milk chocolate and eyes like emeralds. She greets Evian with a huge smile and Evian says something unintelligible back, so I assume they already know each other.

Then we get in the rental car and take off toward the police station. I sit in the front seat and I'm yet again studying the city of Toulouse around me.

But this time I'm not staring at the changes, noting how much time has passed. I'm noting the changes so that I have as much information on the city as possible. My mind is back in police officer mode, and it's not happy with lacking knowledge of the terrain we're working in.

So I take note of the fact that quite a bit of work has been done on the neighborhood around the train station. Despite the grand three-story stone buildings, this still won't be one of the most sought-after neighborhoods in the city, but it also doesn't look as dangerous as it was during my time. People can probably walk through here at night and not look over their shoulders every few seconds. A couple of prostitutes are still out, and one of them no more than fifty meters from a primary school that will open its doors in less than thirty minutes, but Evian doesn't even look her way and I'm tempted to make the same assessment. It's not great that they're there, but it's also not a danger to anyone right now.

I don't see many police officers on the streets—in fact, I only see two, who are talking to a group of homeless guys with at least five dogs in tow—but I spot at least ten guys in uniform writing out parking tickets. There are also quite a few surveillance cameras. I'm not sure if there are many of them here because the neighborhood has been tagged as dangerous or if it's a widespread thing across the entire city.

Despite being so early in the morning, there's a lot of traffic. This is certainly something that has changed a lot in the last thirty years. I guess the city has grown but the infrastructure hasn't been able to follow. The streets are as narrow as when they were built decades ago. I can't even imagine what it will be like trying to drive through this area during rush hour.

We follow Evian as she parks her car in the police station parking lot and walks to her office. It turns out she has one of dozens of desks in an open-plan area, which surprises me at first.

"I thought she was some big-shot investigator from Paris," Clothilde says as she runs a hand along the edge of Evian's mostly empty desk. "Why doesn't she have one of the big offices?"

I shrug. "Well, for one, she's a visitor, theoretically here for only a short time, so it doesn't make sense to kick someone out of their office to make room for her. Also, she's here to investigate the work of fellow officers, so they might not *want* to give her any perks. *Or…*" I trail off as I wrap my mind around this idea. "Or whoever brought her here wants her to be close to the people she's investigating, so they're putting her desk close to theirs, forcing them to interact with her, so to speak."

I glance around the room. Only three desks are occupied. One fortyish woman in uniform is sending angry glances in Evian's direction when she thinks the other woman isn't looking. A man in his early thirties is doing much the same thing from the other side of the room except he's not trying to hide it. At one of the desks closest to Evian, a white-haired woman who must be close to retirement gives Evian a smiling greeting and asks if she wants a cup of coffee.

I'm not sure if it was done on purpose or not, but having Evian here in the open space is definitely good for the job she's here to do.

If I had to guess, I'd say Evian is also happy with the arrangement. She doesn't seem like the type of person who needs a corner office to know her worth, and she'll be spending the majority of her time out in the field, anyway.

"Thank you for offering, Blandine," Evian says to the white-haired colleague. "But I've already had my cup of tea this morning and I don't really like coffee."

Blandine's smile is as grandmotherly as they get. "Of course, Emeline. You just let me know if you change your mind."

"Is Doubira in yet?" Evian asks.

"Oh yes, he came in about half an hour ago. I think some results from that autopsy came in and he took them with him to the green meeting room to read them. Haven't seen him since."

Evian nods and purses her lips. "Sounds like it's an interesting read." She removes her jacket and hangs it on the back of her chair, then takes off toward the far end of the room.

"Oh, come on!" Clothilde cries. "Don't leave us behind like that. We also want to know what the report says."

Evian stops in her tracks. Takes a deep breath.

And comes back for the jacket.

She stares daggers at the pocket where our bones are hiding but wraps the jacket over one arm and takes off toward the green meeting room, grumbling all the way.

SIXTEEN

EMELINE THROWS HER jacket on a chair along the wall when she enters the green meeting room. She tries not to think too hard about why she suddenly decided to bring it with her rather than leave it at her desk.

Malik is sitting at the large table in the middle of the room, with papers spread out to cover almost the entire surface. All the lights are on full blast, making it feel like they're in the middle of a soccer stadium with dozens of floodlights pointed their way. Malik is wearing his usual jeans and white shirt but he has removed his jacket and unbuttoned the top two buttons on his shirt and pushed the sleeves up to his elbows. His short, curly hair is standing up on the left side, where his hand has clearly been running through it a number of times already.

"Are those the autopsy reports?" Emeline asks as she sits down on the chair next to Malik.

He nods. "They came in five minutes after I arrived this morning."

"Nobody else has seen them?"

Malik shakes his head and points to a large brown envelope at the far edge of the table. "They were sealed and addressed to the two of us."

"All right." Emeline takes in the papers strewn across the table. Quite a significant number of pages, if she isn't mistaken. She will sit down and read every word herself later, but if Malik has already gone through everything, she might as well take advantage of it. "Give me the highlights, please."

Malik's eyes widen with a flash of surprise—he must not have expected her to trust his judgment. He recovers quickly, though.

"I guess the most important part is that the DNA from Mademoiselle Humbert's rapist was a match for Gérard de Villenouvelle. The same guy we nailed for the rape and murder of at least six young women in the last few years."

"He might be on trial for the murder," Emeline says softly, "but we actually only have proof that he raped them. There's a very good chance he didn't work alone."

Malik nods, accepting the correction, but doesn't seem to be overly chastened. Good, Emeline doesn't need a partner she has to watch how she talks to.

"Alone or not," Malik continues. "He's been at it for at least thirty years." He pauses and stares at the multitude of papers spread out on the table before him, his lips pressed into a thin line. "Out of those forty bodies we had exhumed, how many do you think were victims of Monsieur de Villenouvelle?"

Emeline was sent down to Toulouse from Paris in order to look into two cold cases. Two mothers were raising hell because they felt their daughters' deaths had been ruled suicides too quickly. Since the integrity of local officers was in question, they asked an outsider to come in and have a look.

It didn't take long to figure out that someone had, indeed, been closing cases too quickly left and right. It wasn't only the two girls whose mothers started the whole thing, either. Emeline easily found thirty-eight different cases of assumed suicides where the police work was sloppy at best.

But she only went back ten years in her search.

Which was the right decision at the time. She needed to catch whoever was killing these girls and it would be easier catching him on the most recent ones, where there might still be evidence on the corpses and where people still might remember the events around the time of death.

"We need to look into all similar cases going back at least thirty years," Emeline says.

Malik's hand goes to a document where Clothilde Humbert's name is written in large block letter at the top. "Do you think Mademoiselle Humbert was his first victim?"

"Probably not. The likeliness of us happening on the very first victim like this is very low. But it does give us a date of reference. We *know* he's been at it for at least this long, so let's focus on the years in between first."

Emeline runs a hand over her face, tired at the mere thought of going through that many files. "Actually, Doubira, you wouldn't happen to know anyone in the building who might be able to help us with this? We need to focus on Mademoiselle Humbert and Monsieur X first."

Malik straightens in his chair and his eyes gleam. "Oh! Uh... yes, I do know someone. A young woman named Nadine Tulle who's scarily good at searching through archives. And she's nice, too. But..." He searches through the scattered papers, discarding everything until he holds one up in triumph. "We know who Monsieur X is!"

Emeline feels the familiar rush of satisfaction she has every time she makes a breakthrough on a case. Then it's topped by whooping joy *and* glee.

Where did those feelings come from?

She's tempted to look over her shoulder because the feeling of having someone looking at her has been pretty much constant since she started working this case, but she refrains. Her colleagues are going to think she's paranoid if she keeps literally looking over her shoulder.

Maybe she *is* becoming paranoid.

Emeline shakes the thought away and reaches for the sheet of paper.

"Robert Villemur," she reads aloud. "Born in 1953, unmarried, no children. Went missing in 1988. He was a police officer." She looks up to meet her colleague's gaze.

Malik nods. "It's probably the only reason we had his DNA on file."

"Any link between him and Mademoiselle Humbert?"

"Yes."

Emeline's head snaps up from where she bent back down to read the document in her hand. "Yes?"

"I asked Nadine to have a quick look when I got the names earlier. She was only able to spend about fifteen minutes on the search, but she did find a link. Lieutenant Robert Villemur was the police officer who investigated Mademoiselle Humbert's death, and ruled it a suicide."

Emeline's eyebrows shoot up and she looks back at the sheet of paper announcing that the exhumed skeleton belonged to Robert Villemur as if it would have an answer to her numerous questions.

"And he was buried right next to her. With no headstone and no official records." She sighs. "A revenge crime?"

Malik lifts his shoulders and blows out his lips to show he doesn't know either, making him look approximately fourteen.

Emeline settles back in her chair, trying to find some calm to let her subconscious think. Sometimes, critical thinking is necessary, to make links and follow logical deductions. But oftentimes, her subconscious did the best work. She just needs to let it do its thing, work with the information she doesn't consciously know she has, make connections that wouldn't make sense to the critical part of her brain.

Her best work was done while staring into space.

This time, though, she gets nothing. Except the need to get moving, do something, figure out what the hell is going on with these killings.

"All right," she says finally, realizing that Malik has let her do her spaced-out thinking in peace. "You can tell me the rest on our way out."

"Where are we going?"

"We're going to visit Robert Villemur's closest relatives."

SEVENTEEN

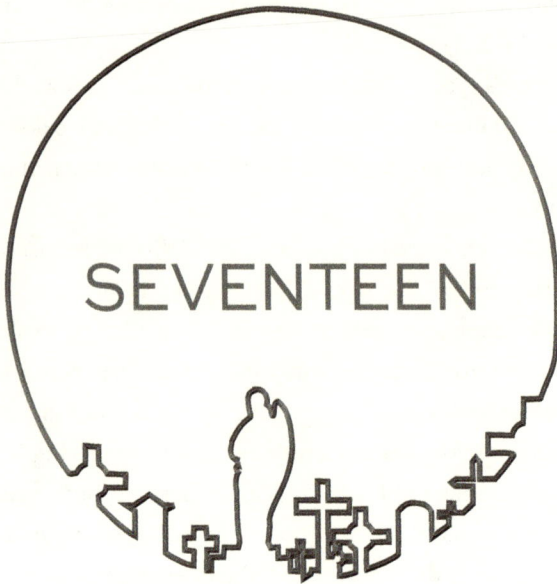

THE RELIEF AT discovering that they managed to identify my body is quickly replaced by worry when they find the fact that I was the police officer to declare Clothilde's death a suicide. I realized this when Clothilde's mother came through our cemetery as a ghost some time ago and she gave me the information I needed to connect the dots, but I never told Clothilde about it.

Now, as I look to her to gauge her reaction, I'm met with an eye roll.

"I already knew."

I freeze. "You knew? How?"

"I remember hearing your name." She shrugs.

"How did you *hear* anything?" My voice is getting ridiculously high. "You were dead!"

Another shrug. "I was already a ghost. Couldn't move more than a centimeter or so away from the body, but I could watch."

"You...but that's not...how on earth..." I shut my mouth with a snap. This girl will never cease to amaze me.

"I'm sorry I failed you," I say finally. "Even though I didn't know you yet, I feel like I failed you as a friend. If I'd done my job correctly, you might not have been stuck in a cemetery for three decades. All those other girls could still be alive."

Clothilde cocks her head and gives me a lopsided smile. "If you'd been a better detective, they wouldn't have put you on the case. They needed someone to confirm it as suicide quickly. That happened to be you."

My mouth falls open. "How...?"

"People don't watch what they say around dead bodies." Clothilde waggles her eyebrows. "Unfortunately, they weren't detailed enough for me to be one hundred percent certain of which of them had actually done the deed. It was either the lawyer or the other guy. Or both."

I'm about to ask for more details when Evian says they're going to see my family.

All thoughts of how bad I was at my job when I was alive fly straight out the window.

I'm not ready.

I haven't seen a single member of my family since I died, and quite a few of them not for years before that. I wasn't the best son, brother, or nephew.

I wonder who they're planning on seeing. Is everybody still alive? Have they changed? Do they remember me? Will it mean anything to them to get confirmation that I'm dead?

The door to the meeting room slams shut behind Evian and Doubira and I'm pulled after them in a manner that's not particularly agreeable. One moment I'm frozen in the meeting room, the next I'm outside the door, watching the two police officers walk down the hall toward the open space where their desks are.

Clothilde is waiting for me in the hallway, leaning a shoulder against the wall and her sharp eyes trained on me. "You okay there, Robert?"

"Yeah." I blow out a long breath. "Moving a bit fast, is all."

She nods. "I'm kind of curious about why they're looking into you first, actually. I'm the one with the obvious ties to their ongoing case." She starts walking after Evian and Doubira and I follow her lead. I'd rather not be pulled around like a puppet with strings again if I can avoid it.

"Maybe that's why," I say. "The mystery of it all. My body clearly wasn't supposed to be down there, so curious minds will want to figure out why. And there is sort of a link between me and the case."

She glances at me as she walks straight through a desk so she can stay on a level with me instead of going in front of or behind me. "You think the link is important? I figured it was happenstance that you were the one to open and shut my case in five seconds flat."

"It could have been. Or I could somehow have been in league with the guy who killed you. Or on the verge of arresting him. Who knows? If there's a link, I think it's a good idea to check it out. In a way, your death is just another dead girl in a long list of dead girls. It helps them set the time line, realize how long this has been going on, but it's not certain it will bring anything else to the table."

We reach Evian's desk. Nobody bothers to sit down—except for Clothilde who jumps up on the grandmotherly officer's desk and starts swinging her legs.

"Where is this Nadine person?" Evian asks Doubira, keeping her voice low so they won't be overheard, or possibly not to bother anyone. "Can we talk to her before we take off?"

"She's one floor down," Doubira replies and whips out his phone from the inside pocket of his jacket. "I'll ask her to come up."

Two minutes later, a tiny woman who barely reaches Evian's shoulders and with a blond braid reaching down to her slim waist strides purposely over to Evian's desk. "How can I help?" she says in lieu of any kind of greeting.

Evian looks her up and down, a slight twitch of her lips the only indication that her first impression of the woman is a good one. "I was told you're the woman to go to if I need some research done?"

Nadine Tulle flashes a smile that should, in any other circumstance, qualify as sweet. But since we're at the police station, and she's in uniform, her no-nonsense style, and the tone of her reply, it comes off as almost predatory. "You've heard right. What do you need?"

Evian hands over two sheets of paper from the autopsy report to the other woman. "Please don't show these to anyone else, or share information with anyone." She raises a hand to stop the offended retort that is clearly on the tip of Tulle's tongue. "I know you won't but it's something I prefer to always say anyway, just in case."

She points to Clothilde's name on one of the reports. "This girl was raped and probably murdered by Gérard de Villenouvelle, the guy who's on trial for the murder of six other girls in the past ten years. You know the case, yes? Clothilde here seems to have suffered the same fate, but thirty years earlier. I want you to search through the intervening years, and find me all the cases that could be the work of the same serial killer."

Spots of color appear on Tulle's cheeks. She's excited about the prospect of looking into this and clearly understands the importance of the task she is given.

"Grandma here is quite interested in that conversation, by the way," Clothilde says. She has moved closer to the elderly police officer, who seems to be engrossed in something on her own computer screen.

"She's been staring at the same thing since we came over here," Clothilde tells me, her gaze flat. "She's either very stupid and can't understand what's in that document she's reading or she's totally eavesdropping."

I turn to Evian to whisper something in her ear to get her to ensure their privacy but she's already on it. With a confused gaze at the grandmotherly officer, she pulls Tulle toward a corner and lowers her voice.

"I also need you to look into this guy," she says and taps a finger on the second sheet of paper. "He was a police officer here thirty years ago and seems to have had *some* sort of link to Clothilde Humbert's demise. I want to know what the link was, who the people he worked with were, if he had any link to de Villenouvelle, everything."

She stares out at the open-plan office, which now is at least half-full, police officers milling to and fro, filing documents, drinking coffee, discussing last night's rugby game, and reading reports.

"I also want to know the names and basic histories of all the officers who were in any way involved in declaring all those young girls' murders as suicides," she says. "Always search for a link with de Villenouvelle."

"Sure thing," Tulle says, nodding quickly, making her braid do a little dance down her back. "Do you want me to call you if I find anything?"

"Call Doubira if you find something you judge urgent," Evian replies. "Otherwise, we'll drop by here again tomorrow morning at the latest to get an update on your progress."

Tulle doesn't waste any more time and with a nod to Doubira she's out the door and on her way down to her own office to start working.

"Seems like you found the right person for the job," Evian says to Doubira as she comes back to her desk. She throws a worried glance at the elderly officer, who is still staring at the same page on her screen, with Clothilde leaning down next to her, pretending to focus just as fiercely on whatever document the woman has open.

Doubira nods but I can see the pride he takes in getting a compliment from his partner. "We trained at ENSOP together. That girl is like a human Google with access to the police database."

"Where are we going?" Evian asks him and pulls on her jacket.

"Uh…" After a short hesitation, Doubira pulls up a page on his phone. "I have the addresses for Villemur's mother, one sister, and two brothers. One brother lives in Bordeaux but the other family members are in Toulouse."

I wonder which brother turned traitor and moved to Bordeaux but most of my brain is fixated on another fact.

My mother's still alive.

"Let's start with the mother," Evian says.

EIGHTEEN

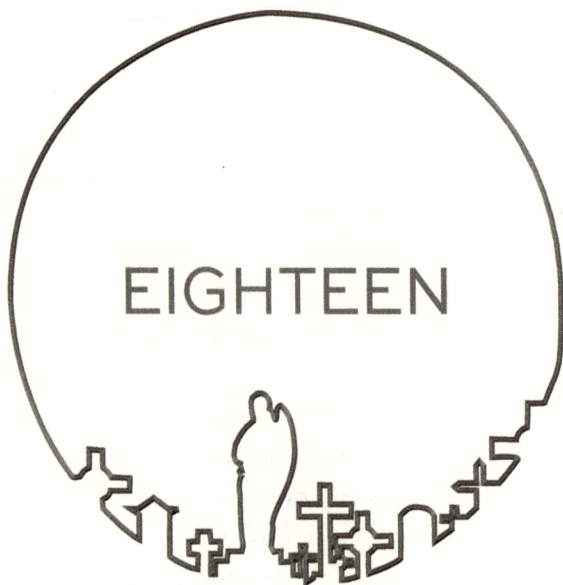

My mom still lives in the same house on the outskirts of the Toulouse city center. The house looks like it hasn't had any maintenance in the last thirty years. The roughcast that used to be off-white is now rather brown, with black tracks below the windows and the gutters. The palm tree next to the garage clearly hasn't had any sort of maintenance in at least a decade. Weeds sprout up in the cracks of the path leading to the front door. And one of the shutters on the second floor has lost all its paint and is hanging off only one of its hinges.

The neighborhood is the same and it isn't. I recognize the streets, the primary school, most of the houses. And then every fifty meters or so, I discover a new apartment building that has shot out of seemingly nothing, making the whole area feel a lot more compact and crowded than it used to be. The pharmacy and post office are still there, but the local supermarket has been replaced with a real estate agent, and the bar around the corner has been walled shut with cinderblocks and I see at least three layers of tags.

I can't believe my mother and siblings let everything fall into disrepair like this. My dad died when I was twenty-one and although it was rough on my mom, she stepped up and did everything around the house like a pro, including house repairs. I do realize that she's much older now—I make a quick calculation and end up on a staggering ninety-one years—but she could have had one of my siblings do it, or paid a professional.

The mom that I knew would have rather died than let this eyesore stand so visibly unattended.

I briefly wonder if the house has perhaps been abandoned, but a light is on at the back of the house, probably in the kitchen. And when Evian rings the doorbell, the light in the living room comes on after a twenty-second lag.

Evian sends a glance at Doubira. "Have you ever done this before?"

"Done what?" The young man looks lost for the first time since I met him.

"Told someone their son is dead."

"Oh." Doubira looks at the door, then at the light behind the curtained window, his mouth hanging open. "You think she…"

"Don't worry," Evian reassures him. "I'll do the talking." She pauses and takes a deep breath. "On an intellectual level, she probably knows her son is dead. But as long as there's no body, the heart usually keeps believing, hoping. It doesn't matter if it's three days after a disappearance or thirty years. It's still going to be difficult news to receive."

I eye the front door with some trepidation. I *have* done this type of house call before. Telling someone that their loved one is dead is *awful*, but I only had to do it with people I didn't know. I had to be the bearer of bad news and suffer their pain, but then I could leave, go back to my job, my life, and more or less push those people's pain away.

But now? I'm standing in front of my own front door, waiting for my own mother to open it. Waiting for Evian to tell her that *I'm* dead.

"You okay, there?" Clothilde asks. She's standing right next to me, her youthful features set into a serious mask. "You flickered."

Like I've seen many other ghosts do when under extreme pressure or when they were particularly emotional.

"I'll be fine," I tell her. I take a deep breath, even though it does me no good since I haven't needed air in thirty years, and square my shoulders.

Clothilde looks down and I follow her gaze. Her hand moves to mine, as if to hold it. She can't, of course, not without my cooperation, since we don't have physical bodies. I play along and open my hand to hers—when we both insist in our minds that the other's hand is real, we can, somewhat, hold onto each other.

And even though I can't *feel* her, it helps.

Finally, after what feels like an eternity but was probably less than two minutes, a clanging of keys sounds behind the door, and the door slowly pulls open.

Maman.

The last time I saw her she was just past sixty. Now she's ninety-one. The difference shows—it's shockingly evident she's now an *old* woman—but she's also still the same.

Her hair is mostly white but there's still a hint of its original dark blond color. Her nose is slightly crooked from when her brother broke it when she was twelve and her eyes are as startlingly blue as I remember. Her movements might be slow, and she's carrying a lot more weight than she used to, but her mind is still sharp.

"What can I do for you, officers?" she asks.

I gulp as her voice brings back a flood of memories. Some good, some bad, but all proving her love for me. At least, that's how I see it now, so many years later.

"We have some news about your son, Robert," Evian says. "Would you mind if we come in?"

My mother shuffles aside while holding the door open, to let Evian and Doubira into the living room, and Clothilde and I follow closely.

"She has your eyes," Clothilde says as she passes my mother. "Or I guess you have hers."

Evian's gaze shoots to my mother's face but I see no reaction on my mother. Guess she's not as sensitive as Evian. Not many people are.

I lift a hand to touch my mother's cheek. It's not something I ever did while I was alive but this might be my last chance and she can't see or feel me anyway. Then I move away to let Evian do her job in peace.

"Robert?" my mother says, her voice cracking.

At first, I think she *did* feel me, but I quickly realize her eyes are on Evian. She *knows* what's coming.

"We recently discovered his body," Evian says. She's kind of cold and distant but also compassionate. She's good at this. "He's been dead for thirty years. I'm so sorry for your loss."

NINETEEN

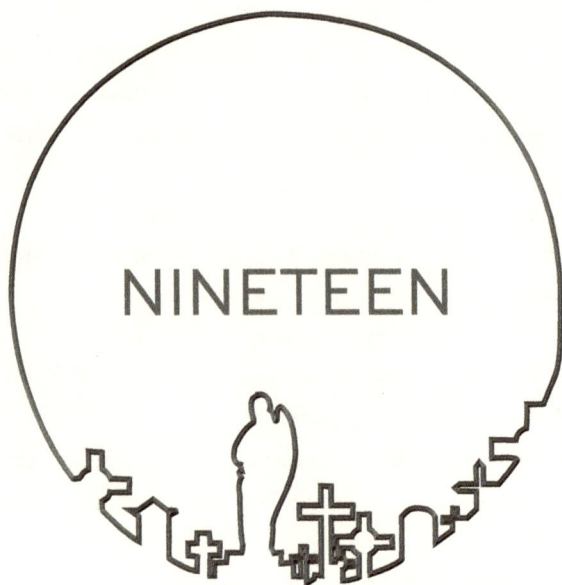

It's VERY SLOW, and almost impossible to see, but my mother is slowly deflating. Her hand, still on the doorknob, tightens so the knuckles turn white and the veins on the back of her hand stand out in stark contrast to her spotted white skin. I can't even put my finger on what is happening exactly, but it's like she's folding in on herself, becoming smaller. My mother, who was always bigger than life itself.

"He died thirty years ago, you say?" she says to Evian and forces herself to release the door and let it swing shut. "When he disappeared?"

"Yes. As of today, we have very few details, I'm afraid, but we wanted to let you know as soon as possible once we identified him. Please rest assured that we're working on figuring out what happened to him."

While Evian talks, Doubira studies the living room around him without leaving his spot next to Evian, and Clothilde as usual has no qualms about snooping around. I'm observant enough to have noticed that the inside of the house hasn't changed much more than the outside has, although it seems to have aged better, but almost all my focus is on my mom. Who is receiving the news of my death, right before my eyes, and I can't even go over and console her.

"You look so young!" Clothilde exclaims. She's studying my official photo from the police force, the one they bring out to show the world when you die in the line of duty. My mom has placed this one in a small niche in the wall that we never understood the point of. Guess she found a use for it in the end.

"I was twenty-four when that was taken," I tell her over my shoulder.

"Still," she mutters. "You look so...innocent."

I wasn't, of course. There's a reason I have so much to atone for before moving on to the afterlife.

My focus is pulled back to my mother as she shuffles over to a rickety chair standing next to the shoe locker. "Where did you find him?" she asks Evian.

"In a cemetery in one of the small villages outside of the city," Evian says, making me wonder why she doesn't give the name of the village.

"He was buried in a cemetery?"

Evian tips her head with a grimace. "Not officially. There is no record of anyone being buried there, but we happened upon his casket when we exhumed the body next to his."

93

My mother's gray eyebrows shoot up and I see a glimmer of the attitude I remember so well. "You *happened* on his casket when you were exhuming *someone else*? Who was this someone?"

"I'm afraid I can't divulge that information right now," Evian replies smoothly. "Not until we figure out what the link was between the two murders—if indeed there is a link."

"Murders." My mother still looks old, still looks defeated, but there's steel in her eyes and I can *feel* her ready to fight for her son. For me. "Robert was murdered, then."

Evian shrugs, making me think that wasn't a slip of the tongue. She wants my mother to know. "He was buried illegally in an unmarked grave. Chances are he was murdered." She pauses for a moment, debating something with herself. "Of course, the bullet lodged in his spine is also a good indication."

My mother pulls herself up a little straighter. "You have the bullet that killed my boy?"

Evian nods.

"You will investigate his murder? You will find him justice?"

My heart swells to see my mother caring about me like this. It should be obvious that a mother loves her children, but sometimes, when you get caught up in your life and its problems and ups and downs, it's easy to lose sight of it. Easy to wonder if your family does, in fact, love you.

Seeing it now, even thirty years too late, lifts a weight off my chest that I hadn't even realized was there.

"I will investigate," Evian replies calmly. "I cannot make any promises. The murder took place a very long time ago and we have very few leads. But I *will* do my best. That I can promise."

My mother studies her for a moment, her gaze piercing. Then she nods. "Thank you," she says. She looks around as if searching for something but her gaze never settles anywhere. Until she catches sight of my picture in that niche.

"Does this mean I can finally bury my son?" she asks.

Evian nods. "We'll need a few more days to make sure we've gotten all the information we need from the remains, but yes, it means you can organize his funeral."

I've been dead for over thirty years and have attended a vast number of funerals during my time in the cemetery, so I wouldn't think having my own funeral arranged—so late—would mean anything to me. And in a way it doesn't. But seeing the peace this will bring to my mother, seeing the unshed tears she's fighting to hold back while there are strangers in her house, makes me realize it will mean something *to her*. And that means it will mean something to me.

I walk over and put a hand on my mother's shoulder, giving it a squeeze.

Clothilde, of course, chooses this moment to speak up. "Do you think she'll use this god-awful picture at the funeral?"

TWENTY

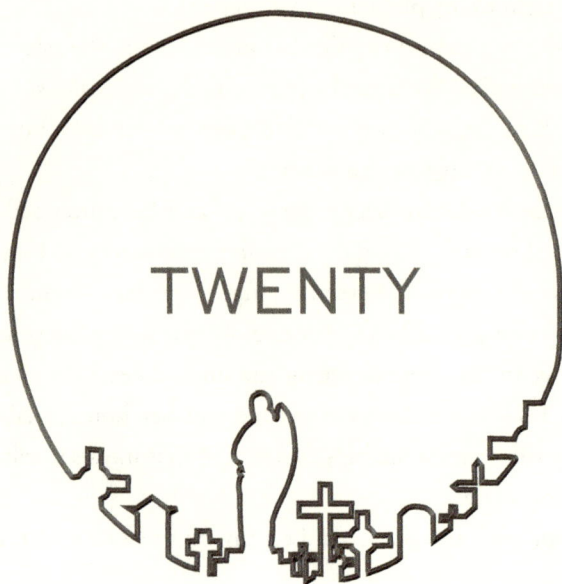

EMELINE GIVES MADAME Villemur the time she needs to get over the worst of her shock. No matter how long the man's been missing, there was always a vague hope that he was still alive somewhere. He could have been kidnapped, or decided to up and leave everything and everyone behind to start a new life somewhere else. Still, it was more likely that the man was dead, especially considering his line of work. So on some level, Madame Villemur probably suspected her son was dead, but now she has firm confirmation.

All things considered, she comes around quickly. And when she does, she offers her visitors some coffee.

"Could you tell us a little about your son?" Emeline asks as she sits down at the kitchen table while Madame Villemur shuffles over to the coffee machine and takes out three mugs from an overhead cupboard. "Knowing him and his history could help us in our search for his killer."

The woman sighs and runs her hands over her hips. She's wearing a pair of brown slacks and a black button-down shirt. Her glasses are surprisingly in fashion—round on the bottom and with a slim black rim—and her hair is immaculately made up in that short voluminous hairdo so many elderly ladies seem to favor. This is someone for whom keeping up appearances is important but not in a gaudy over-the-top kind of way.

"Robert was always the difficult child," she says. "We did our best, but it's possible we paid him less attention than his brothers and sister. He wasn't the oldest, he wasn't the youngest, he wasn't the only girl. He was also very independent and didn't want to share much of his life with us, from a very early age."

She pours three cups of coffee and sinks into a chair across from Emeline. She keeps her eyes on her own cup, holding it as if seeking warmth. "I was very surprised when he told us he wanted to become a police officer. He was always the one to search for loopholes in the rules or to downright break them if he thought he could get away with it. Respecting authority wasn't really his thing."

Emeline feels some surprise to discover this even though there's no obvious reason for it. The only link they have between Robert Villemur and Clothilde Humbert is that he was the one to declare her death a suicide—which *could* indicate that he was a dirty cop.

Except that isn't the impression Emeline has of him—for whatever reason.

"Still," Madame Villemur continues, "he was happy while attending the officers' school and seemed to make friends. I'm not quite certain how a police officer's career progresses usually, but it seemed to me he was moving up in the ranks at a respectable rate."

"Did he ever talk to you about the cases he worked on?" Emeline asks.

Madame Villemur shakes her head. "Nothing specific. Hardly anything at all, really, except to say it was going well and that they were keeping him busy." She huffs a mirthless laugh. "Just like when he was ten and I asked him how his day had been at school. 'It was fine.' Never any details, not even to tell me what subject they were working on."

The old woman finally takes a sip of her coffee and Emeline follows suit. Although she doesn't like coffee, she never refuses a cup when interviewing on the job. She has learned to force the stuff down when needed. Malik, on the other hand, seems to be savoring the black brew, taking regular small sips and holding the mug close to his nose to inhale the scent even when he's not drinking. His eyes are bright and he's following the conversation closely, though.

Emeline brings a hand below the table to touch the two bones in her pocket. She still doesn't understand the strong urge she has to keep them with her at all times but she won't fight it. She feels a connection to these two people who have been dead for over thirty years and wants to help them get justice. A talisman or two won't hurt anybody.

Even though she doesn't really know more than the age and name of Clothilde, it's Robert Villemur who is the big mystery. Why was he killed? Why was he buried next to Clothilde and not dumped in a forest somewhere? What role, if any, did he play in Clothilde's murder?

"I'm not quite sure how to phrase this," she says, making sure she makes eye contact with Madame Villemur. "But do you think there is any chance your son was involved in anything illegal?"

Madame Villemur stares back, her face serious. "What kind of illegal activities are we talking about?"

"I'm not even sure. And I have absolutely no proof at this time. I'm simply trying to get a feel for his character, I guess. If you tell me you're certain he was into drug trafficking or blackmail, then I would start out working on certain assumptions. I'm not saying I would take anything you say for granted, either positive or negative, but it would help me find a starting point."

In any case, Emeline would have to look into both scenarios. Right now, it seemed equally probable that he was killed because he was partly to blame for Clothilde Humbert's murder and was buried next to her as some sort of vengeance, or because he was investigating the murder and came too close to the truth and therefore had to disappear. Still, the man's mother's opinion would be interesting to have, especially presented in a way that should make her want to push Emeline toward thinking her son was innocent.

Madame Villemur takes a few minutes to contemplate her answer. "I don't see how he could have taken part in any drug trafficking scheme. It's too dangerous and stressful. Robert was too lazy for that."

She takes another sip of her coffee. "Blackmail? I guess that's possible—but once again that implies a certain level of risk-taking and that just doesn't sound like my son." She sighs deeply. "He always took the road of least resistance. If there was a way to avoid doing the work but still get the prize, he would be on it in a heartbeat. It's why I was so surprised when he wanted to train to be a police officer. I never had the impression it's a particularly easy profession?"

Emeline snorts a laugh at that. "Not really, no, although I guess it's possible to slack off anywhere, even at ENSOP. Once you start working, it's certainly possible, if you're not set on having a brilliant career."

"Hmm." Madame Villemur's gaze shifts from Emeline to Malik and back again. "But he did seem to be on some sort of career path. I believe he was going places. Maybe he finally grew up and developed a professional conscience."

Maybe. Or he had some sort of help to rise in the ranks.

"My Robert got in real trouble only once during his time in school," Madame Villemur says, fixing Emeline with her eyes. "It was in ninth grade and some of the 'cool' boys pulled him along on a nocturnal excursion into the school to vandalize the headmaster's office. Needless to say, they got caught and were all suspended for a week and had to clean up the office themselves.

"Now, Robert would never have had such an idea by himself. I'm not saying he was an innocent boy who would never do anything stupid, simply that he'd never get the idea or take the initiative. Now, what he *would* do, was to follow the lead of others. The leader of that group promised friendship and status, and Robert followed him blindly."

Madame Villemur sets her cup down and plants both palms on each side of it. "Robert wouldn't have gotten in trouble by himself, on his own initiative. But I wouldn't be the least bit surprised if someone else tempted him with a promotion or some cash and that he followed blindly after a leader, just like in ninth grade."

This *could* be a mother who desperately tries to protect her deceased son's reputation. But Emeline doesn't think that's the case. She thinks Madame Villemur knew her son pretty well and that her theory is sound.

She'll look into other possibilities too, of course. But her gut tells her this is an accurate description of Robert Villemur and her gut is rarely wrong.

TWENTY-ONE

I'M NOT GONNA lie—hearing my mother's opinion of my character hurt. Your mother is supposed to love you no matter what, believe in you when nobody else does, and always defend you if someone attacks you. What my mother just did can most definitely qualify as throwing me under the proverbial bus.

Except she's right.

That business in ninth grade? I would never have been the instigator of such action, or someone to push it as a good idea. But I *did* follow the "cool" kids into it with my eyes wide open because they promised me I'd be one of them if I did.

And clearly I'm particularly stupid because I'm not even able to learn from my past mistakes. The cool guys in my class didn't bring me into their fold. I didn't even *want* them to after we got caught. I realized they were bad news and would only get me into more trouble.

And yet, when a similar opportunity presented itself a few years later, I jumped at it.

A couple of guys I was hanging out with wanted to become police officers, with the logic that if they were part of the police, they wouldn't get caught by the police when they did whatever shady stuff they were up to at the time. I didn't even question it, didn't ask them what this illegal business they were clearly mixed up with was, or wonder how the police managed it when the bad guy was one of their own.

I just followed blindly and signed up for the officers' school.

I somehow lost contact with those guys while we were in training. But I picked up new "idols."

And that was the first step that would finally lead me to Clothilde's murder scene.

"Were you really like that?" Clothilde asks me, bringing me back to the present. She's studying me more intently than I can remember her ever doing, as if trying to see the miserable being my mother describes.

"Unfortunately, yes," I tell her. I'm keeping my eyes on Evian, trying to gauge her reaction to my mother's stories. When I confirm to Clothilde, I see a twitch in Evian's eyes that makes me believe she heard me. She'll be working under the assumption that I was a loser who blindly followed other people into trouble.

Which I was, so I'll try not to complain.

"You're not anymore." Clothilde doesn't phrase this as a question but as a statement.

I start to roll my eyes as I look up to meet her gaze. She's not usually someone who likes to state the obvious. But before I can get the words out, I realize she's telling *me* I'm not like that anymore.

"I know that," I say with annoyance. Except…it does feel good to have my one and only close friend state so forcefully that I'm no longer the loser I used to be. So I take a deep breath I don't need and add, "Thank you."

Clothilde's eyes twinkle and she winks at me. "My pleasure, Robert."

The discussion between Evian and my mother goes on for a while longer but none of it tells me anything I didn't already know. I keep glancing around the living room of the house I grew up in and it's making me antsy. I think part of me wants to revert to the idiot I was when I lived here, that the setting is bringing back old reflexes.

When Evian finally thanks my mother for the coffee—even though she hardly touched it—I'm more relieved than I want to admit. After Evian and Doubira both shake hands with my mother, I take the liberty of giving my mother a hug before the door shuts and I'll be pulled out after Evian.

I might not get another opportunity, and I hope that if my mother is the slightest little bit sensitive to otherworldly activities, she'll know on a certain level that I love her and miss her.

I catch sight of a single tear making its way across her wrinkled cheek as the door clicks shut and I'm forcefully pulled out.

This time I don't even wince.

TWENTY-TWO

"WHERE TO NOW, boss?" Doubira asks when they get into Evian's car and Clothilde and I settle in the back.

"I'm not your boss, Doubira," Evian says with a smile. "We're partners."

"Right." Doubira sends her a sideways glace and his lips lift in a slight smile. "If you say so, *partner*. So where to?"

I can tell Evian is fighting a smile of her own. In a way, Doubira is right. Between the two of them, she's definitely the one in charge, the one sent down here from Paris to look into a series of murders, and Doubira is just along for the ride. However, Doubira should not take that to assume he can't take the initiative and make decisions on his own. He'll be of no use to his partner if he simply tags along like a lost puppy without ever questioning what they're doing.

"We need to figure out if there was some link between Robert Villemur and Gérard de Villenouvelle. That man is the main connection we have between Clothilde's murder and the ones happening recently in a very similar manner. He was a bad cop. He was working in Toulouse when Clothilde died. And Villemur had the potential to be a bad cop—or at least to be led astray by one."

I feel the need to tell her I'm not a bad cop but manage to keep silent. I don't want to influence her opinion on this. And she's most likely onto something.

I don't remember working with or for this Gérard de Villenouvelle but that doesn't mean there was no link. I know I followed the instructions of several people I never knew well enough to learn their names. Someone who'd promised me something told me to do what they said, so I did.

Doubira acts as guide as Evian drives us back to the police station. I stare out the window but make no effort to take note of the scenery like I did on the way over.

After five minutes, Clothilde whispers, so as not to be overheard by Evian's subconscious: "Hey, Robert? Do you think there *was* a link between you and de Villenouvelle?"

I turn to study her. Clothilde's most common expression is that of a bored teenager, a look I'm so used to, I consider it her norm. Right now there's no teenager in sight. What I see is a worried and serious young woman who's wondering if her friend of thirty years had anything to do with the night she died. I'm guessing she'd forgive me if I *was* guilty but I hope we'll never come to that.

And that's a big part of my problem. "I don't really remember the last days I was alive," I whisper back. "I don't remember taking that bullet and I don't remember anyone who might have wanted to pull the trigger on me."

I put my ghostly hand on hers on the seat between us. "What I can tell you is that the name Gérard de Villenouvelle doesn't ring any bells at all. So if I heard it while I lived, it was during those last days that I've lost. I certainly never heard it before going to that hotel room and declaring your death a suicide."

"Why *did* you do that?" We never did get around to discussing my motivations, partly because she probably assumed I was as upstanding alive as I was dead.

Dying and becoming a ghost really *can* change a man.

"I was as spineless as my mother described," I say, vaguely noting we're getting closer to the police station but that the traffic is very slow. "I was always following someone's orders, preferably someone who promised me easy advancement as long as I followed their instructions.

"The guy who told me to go to that hotel room hadn't been around for long but he'd already hooked his claws in me. If I did what he said, I'd make captain in no time. It wasn't even a threat or promise, he just presented it as fact. He was the ideal captain and if he put in a good word with the bosses, I was sure to follow in his footsteps. So I took his words for gospel. I think I closed three other cases without really looking at the evidence before getting to that hotel room."

I run a hand down my face as the memories flood back. I see the gaudy hotel room, the girl spreadeagled on the bed with both her wrists slit, and the blood soaking into the carpet, making it difficult to get close to the scene without stepping on evidence.

"I didn't even really look at your face when I was there," I whisper, unable to meet my friend's gaze. "I was told it was a suicide, so I saw only the elements that pointed in that direction, and put my signature on the report by the end of the day. I never even learned your name."

"Well, you know it now." Clothilde's voice is gentle and I can't believe how lucky I am to have her for a friend. "What was the name of this guy who was giving you orders?"

"Montbleu," I say. I allow my voice to carry a little now. If the name somehow makes its way into Evian's subconscious so she'll react the next time she hears it, all the better. "Pierre Montbleu."

"Okay. Good." Clothilde taps out a short rhythm on her thighs. "We'll keep our eyes and ears open for the name and make sure to scream our heads off when we see it."

I can't help but laugh at the idea—but it's also true. Evian is so sensitive that I think if we both start to panic around her, she'll feel it.

The question is, will she be able to act on the feeling?

TWENTY-THREE

WHEN WE ARRIVE at the police station, it's time for lunch. I expect Evian to declare they'll be eating a sandwich at their desks, but she surprises me—and apparently Doubira if his expression is anything to go by—and tells Doubira to invite Tulle and find the three of them a nice restaurant not too far away. She doesn't want to get back in traffic and I silently thank her for it. This is something that has definitely gotten worse in the last thirty years.

Doubira chooses a classic *brasserie* less than two hundred meters from the station and all five of us take off on foot, Doubira and Tulle up front reminiscing about their not so distant days in training, and Evian behind, unknowingly flanked by two ghosts.

Evian seems to be listening in on the conversation between Doubira and Tulle but I don't think she's interested in the specifics of any of the anecdotes the two mention. She's trying to get to know them, to understand their characters, to make sure she can trust them.

The *brasserie* is in a small whitish house from the fifties with red tiles and blue shutters, squeezed in between two modern four-floor apartment buildings. Several tables are crowded into a covered patio up front, squeezed in between the house and the busy street, but most of the seating is upstairs. The police officers are allowed to choose their table, and they go with the one closest to the restrooms—because a cupboard separates it somewhat from the other tables.

Tulle seems to have understood this is a working lunch because the minute everybody has ordered, she pulls a tablet out of her purse and opens up a document loaded with information.

"I've only had a few hours so far," she says, "so the information I'm giving you now is the stuff that anyone could have found for you. It's just a question of typing in the right questions in the police search engine." Her long blond braid hangs across her right breast and as she finishes her statement, she grabs it and throws it over her shoulder to get it out of the way. I think she doesn't like making a report so soon and wants to make it clear to Evian that she's capable of more than what she can show right now.

"I wasn't expecting you to have solved our dozens of cold murder cases in one morning," Evian reassures her with a smile. "That would mean everyone else, Doubira here and myself included, is absolute shit at their jobs, after all."

Tulle cracks a smile at this and twists her head in a way that brings the braid back to the front. Doubira follows the movement with his eyes—I do believe he likes the braid.

The waiter arrives with a bottle of water and he walks right through Clothilde as he places it on the table. She looks up at him in annoyance but doesn't bother to move. The police officers are at a table for four so there was one unoccupied chair. I tried to offer it to Clothilde when we first arrived but she preferred to sit on a pretend chair at the end of the table. I appreciate the gesture, as she's much more at ease than me at sitting on things that aren't there in the real world.

The waiter must have felt her annoyance, because he scurries off a lot faster than he should have.

While Evian pours water for everyone, Tulle taps on her screen. "Well, here's what I got so far. I have the list of all women between the ages of sixteen and twenty-five who died in this entire region during the period you asked for. Then I have marked the ones who were ruled as suicide. I've flagged the ones that seem to be legit because there was precedence of depression or other attempts and/or suicide notes. I have the names of the officers who signed the reports for all the cases where the police was involved. There's a different flag when the family made enough fuss about their kids not being prone to suicide to make it into the official reports."

Tulle looks up to meet Evian's eyes. "Gérard de Villenouvelle does not appear in any of the reports. If he was involved, he managed to stay in the shadows."

Evian nods. "He was involved but clearly not *that* stupid."

"Do any names appear several times?" Doubira asks. He's sitting sideways in his chair so he can stretch his legs out next to the table. The man is tall and wiry and looks like he should be playing basketball, or maybe soccer.

Tulle runs a hand down her braid as she answers. "Yes, several pairs of partners were responsible for declaring some of the suicides. Never more than two or three, though, and usually over a period of several years. I've extracted the information for you—I'll send you the file as soon as I get back to the office."

"What about a Robert Villemur?" Evian says and I jump a little in my seat at hearing my own name—not that it should be a surprise at this point. "Is that a name that came up anywhere?"

"Well, we know he was the one to declare Clothilde's death a suicide." Tulle bends over her tablet and taps furiously. Her eyebrows shoot up. "He signed off on *two* suicides in the late eighties. One of them was Clothilde Humbert, the other Gisèle Grand."

This information makes my non-beating heart speed up. I have no memory of a Gisèle Grand. In fact, I have no memory of investigating any suicides other than Clothilde's. Is it really possible that I *forgot* about working on the case?

"When did Mademoiselle Grand die?" Doubira asks.

"Two weeks after Mademoiselle Humbert," Tulle replies immediately. She taps some more on her tablet. Raises her eyes to stare first at Doubira, then at Evian. "Two days before he was reported missing, never to be seen again."

Oh. I meet Clothilde's surprised look across the table. I had worked on a case similar to hers just before I died? During the period that I have no memory of?

It makes the guilt rise in my chest to know that I've probably deprived yet another family of the closure they needed after the death of their loved one. That because of me, a killer is walking free. But I manage to push the feelings aside. I need to focus on the positive in this situation—the fact that it's a very good clue and something that needs to be looked into.

"Guess I know where we're going next," Evian says lightly. She leans back as the waiter arrives with the starters—a goat cheese feuilleté that makes me regret not having taste buds—and they all stop talking shop until the man has left.

"Could you scare up an address for Mademoiselle Grand's next of kin?" Evian asks Tulle as she pushes the first forkful of feuilleté into her mouth.

"Of course," Tulle replies briskly, apparently offended that someone would think it *possible* that she couldn't find such information. "You'll have it in your inbox as soon as we're back at the station."

She leans over her plate and therefore misses the look that Evian shares with Doubira. Evian is happy with Tulle's expertise and competence. This isn't the last time they'll ask her for assistance.

I turn to tell Clothilde I share the sentiment but I'm stopped short by the expression on her face. She's centimeters from Doubira's plate and the envy and want she's emanating is downright painful to watch.

"I miss food," she whispers.

"Me too," I tell her.

"I miss goat cheese."

I sigh. This isn't an issue I had at all anticipated when we escaped the cemetery. Nobody ever eats when they visit graves in a cemetery. So we were never exposed to this kind of temptation.

Now I suspect we'll just have to get used to it.

Clothilde tries to steal the food from Doubira's fork before he puts in it his mouth but the whole thing simply goes straight through her ghostly form.

She sniffs and juts her lower lip out in a pout. "Goat cheese!"

TWENTY-FOUR

MADEMOISELLE GRAND'S SISTER lives on the other side of the city center from the police station. Emeline has absolutely no wish to get back into the car and suffer the traffic but she's equally loathe to use public transportation. She's tempted to ask Doubira if the police around here often use the sirens when they don't strictly need it but shoves the thought away. There isn't much she finds more annoying than abusing one's power.

They're visiting the sister because the parents are long dead. The mother passed away mere years after her daughter and the father suffered a heart attack about ten years ago. Mademoiselle Grand leaves one divorced sister and three nephews and nieces that she never got the chance to meet.

When Doubira had the woman on the phone earlier, he didn't give much information but had to admit it was about her sister before the woman would agree to see them. Her distrust of the police could be due to general distrust of all strangers, or because of a specific incident—like the mismanagement of her sister's death.

Emeline won't be able to confirm to the woman that her sister was murdered until they exhume the body but, a quick check of Tulle's file showed a red tag next to Gisèle Grand. The family had put up a fuss and strongly disagreed with the possibility that their girl had decided to take her own life.

Mademoiselle Grand succumbed to the same murderer as Clothilde, Manon, Lise, and at least four other girls, Emeline is certain of it.

The traffic is as bad as expected but they keep themselves occupied. Doubira reads the main results of Tulle's preliminary report out loud. None of the names, belonging to victims or lack-luster police officers, ring any bells—except for Robert Villemur, of course.

Emeline also finds herself marveling at the city around her, which is rather odd. She has never been in this part of the city before, so why is she so surprised to find a large mall in an area that Doubira informs her used to be a textile factory?

At a little past four, they stand on the third floor landing of a newish apartment building, knocking at a door indicating that one Grand and three Guillaume-Grands live there, complete with drawings that Emeline hopes were made by someone below the age of three.

A dark-skinned boy, who looks to be about five, opens the door and without saying a word he peers up at them with large, brown eyes.

115

"Hello, young man," Doubira says, squatting down to be on the boy's level. "Is your mom at home? I think she's expecting us."

Emeline breathes out a relieved sigh. Doubira seems to be good with children. She'll make sure to put him on the front line whenever they have to interact with the little monsters.

A second head pops out behind the door. This time a girl, probably eight or nine. Basically a taller and more female version of the first kid. "What do you want?" she asks with a frown.

Doubira straightens from his squat, making him loom over the girl, but he pastes on a large smile. It makes him look so much younger. "We're here to talk to your mother. Is she home?"

The girl studies Doubira from head to toe, taking in his clothes, but if Emeline isn't mistaken, also his skin color, so similar to her own. "She didn't do anything wrong."

"I know she didn't," Doubira says calmly. "We have some questions for her, but nothing that can get her into any kind of trouble, promise. I think she'll *want* to hear what we have to say."

"Why?"

"Just go get your mom," Emeline cuts in. It's a bit curt, but she doesn't have time to stand around here in the hallway all day, waiting for a kid to give her permission to talk to her mom.

In the end, nobody needs to get the mom—she shows up on her own. She's about Emeline's height, has shoulder-length blond hair and blue eyes and wears a pair of worn jeans and a billowing white shirt. "Evian and Doubira?" she asks as she studies us. "Can I see some ID, please?"

They both show their IDs. Emeline isn't certain if the woman would have recognized a fake one if she saw it but she's happy the woman doesn't let any random stranger into her home.

"Why don't you guys go into the kitchen and have your *goûter*?" Madame Grand says to her two children, pushing their heads gently in the direction she wants them to go. Whenever someone brings up the similarities between having pets and raising kids, the parents always get insulted. But *that* is definitely herding.

"But I can't reach the glasses!" the small boy complains.

"Go get your sister from her room—she can help you. Now *zou*." Again, she gives them a push and this time they follow directions. Madame Grand follows a few steps behind and closes the kitchen door with a soft click.

She gestures to our left. "Why don't you come into the living room. This is about Gisèle?"

We enter the small living room. At first Emeline can't figure out where to sit because of all the toys—they're in the bookcase, on the table, on the couch, on the floor, behind the curtain—but Madame Grand makes quick work of the mess on the couch and gestures for Emeline and Malik to sit.

"I realize our showing up here might be a little bit of a surprise," Emeline says. She sits straight on the couch, her elbows on her knees and her hands folded.

"We saw our fair share of police officers in the day," Madame Grand says, her voice so calm Emeline is sure she's holding back her anger. "But once they'd said their piece and closed down every effort on our part to get justice for Gisèle, they disappeared and never came back." She raises one elegant eyebrow. "One could say you're thirty years late."

Emeline doesn't show her annoyance at having been interrupted. In a way she can understand why the woman wants to lash out at them—except it quite clearly wasn't Emeline or Malik's fault that Gisèle didn't get justice. Emeline was barely seven at the time and Malik wasn't even born.

"We *are* thirty years late," Emeline agrees with a tight smile. "I'm looking into a case that has a very wide reach, and your sister's death was mentioned in one of the reports."

"What is this case of yours about? What's the link with Gisèle?"

"I'm afraid I can't tell you the details of the ongoing case."

Madame Grand snorts and takes a breath to say something undoubtedly scathing but Emeline doesn't let her.

"I *cannot* tell you about the other case unless it's proven that it's in direct relation to your sister's death. And even then I might have to keep certain facts back. I don't particularly like lying so I try to avoid it. This is me being honest about the fact that I'll be keeping things from you. If you want us to look into Gisèle's death, this is the deal. Take it or leave it."

Madame Grand takes her time considering Emeline's offer. Her face gives away nothing, except for a wince when it sounds like something broke in the kitchen. She stares at Emeline so intently Emeline feels like the woman must be seeing every single one of her buried secrets. She fights the urge to fidget and stares right back at the other woman.

"You keep saying 'Gisèle's death,'" she says. "The others always said 'Gisèle's suicide.' Always, without fail. As if saying it often enough would make it true."

Emeline starts nodding then catches herself. "I don't know enough about the case or about your sister to have an opinion on that yet." She holds up a hand when Madame Grand takes a breath to interrupt again. "You telling me over and over that it *wasn't* suicide won't have much effect either."

Madame Grand huffs a laugh at this and leans back in her chair. Looks like she'll let Emeline talk.

"The only thing I know right now is that your sister's name popped up in a report regarding a different crime. Now, Gisèle's name didn't mean anything to me, but the name of the first officer on the scene did. His name was Robert Villemur."

Emeline leaves a pause, hoping the other woman will react to the name.

Madame Grand frowns slightly as she tries to get the name to ring a bell. "I don't...that's not one of the officers we had to talk to when we asked them to look closer at the crime scene, the body, or the hotel."

Emeline's breath catches. She also died in a hotel room? This seems to be a definite pattern. She glances at Malik, who is already bent over his phone.

"I'm asking Nadine to add death location to the report."

Madame Grand is so lost in her own memories she doesn't even seem to have caught the exchange between Emeline and Malik. "I have a cousin named Robert," she says. "I'd have remembered that name."

Her eyes suddenly focus and she leans forward, pointing a finger at Emeline. "I *do* remember that name, but not in relation to Gisèle. Is that the officer who went missing?"

Emeline freezes. She doesn't want to give anything away by reacting too strongly but there's a good chance she gives herself away by the lack of reaction instead.

"An officer went missing?" she asks.

Madame Grand nods. Her eyes dart between Emeline and Malik, clearly picking up every little clue they might let slip. "I don't remember the exact date when the story hit the papers because we were otherwise occupied because of Gisèle. Nothing really registered right then. But it wasn't long after her death. That's why I remember it without really remembering it." She nods firmly. "The officer who went missing was definitely named Robert. No clue about the last name, I'm afraid."

Malik is still bent over his phone, squinting at it while reading some text that was clearly not meant for such a small screen. He looks up at Emeline, his mouth slightly agape.

"August thirteenth," he says. He shakes himself as he realizes nobody understands what he's talking about. "Robert Villemur was declared missing on August thirteenth 1988."

"Gisèle died on August eleventh," Madame Grand whispers.

Well, then. *Looks like we have a clue.*

TWENTY-FIVE

I'M *REALLY* LIKING those new telephones. I have yet to see anyone use it to actually call anyone—that all seems to have been replaced with sending off short, instant messages and getting replies within minutes. And now, Doubira used it to find thirty-year-old articles concerning my disappearance in mere moments.

What I wouldn't have given to have such a tool at my disposal when I was an active police officer.

I hadn't even thought about the possibility of my death or disappearance making the news. But it makes sense—even for a guy as unpopular as me. Not only did I disappear without a trace—I'm reading the article over Doubira's shoulder—but I was, after all, a police officer. When one goes missing, it's easy to assume that something nefarious has happened.

And we don't want the public to think that crimes against police officers will go unpunished.

Clothilde is leaning over Doubira right next to me—it's a good thing he's not as sensitive as Evian or he'd be freaking out right now—but when he presses a button on the side and the screen goes black, she steps over to the table littered with toys and jumps up to sit in her signature way with her legs dangling. She has chosen to ignore the toys and lets them go through her slightly translucent body.

"You don't remember this girl at all?" she asks me.

I shake my head. "I remember you. Seeing your dead body, writing the horribly incomplete report. But I don't remember doing it a second time."

I purse my lips as I keep shaking my head. "Two so similar deaths so close together should have made alarm bells go off. Even to the guy I was back then."

Clothilde cocks her head and I can feel her gaze all the way to the bottom of my soul as she searches for answers. "I can't wrap my mind around you being such a loser when you were alive. You were always so serious in the cemetery, taking care of everyone, making sure everybody found what they needed. How could you have been an incompetent idiot who followed the orders of bullies mere weeks before I first met you?"

I step away from Doubira and Evian as their interview with Madame Grand continues. I don't want our discussion to influence theirs, or to bring Evian too much confusion. She reacts every time we say something in her presence—I won't let it get in the way of her investigation.

"There *was* a time lapse between the police officer that I used to be and the ghost you know me as," I say to Clothilde. "There's a lapse for everyone, it's just of a duration depending on the deceased."

"When you were screaming your head off in the casket?" She cracks half a smile, clearly enjoying making fun of my panic thirty years ago.

I know her well enough to not be the least offended, though. This is Clothilde being playful.

"Yes, when I was screaming. We all do. It's natural. You wake up in a horribly enclosed space, doesn't take long to conclude it's a casket. You think you've been buried alive." Actually, it's more believing that you're in the process of being buried alive. Most of the time, the ghosts wake up in the casket during the ceremony in church. So they'll "feel" the casket being carried out of the church, across the cemetery, and lowered into the ground.

Don't get me started on the sound of dirt hitting the casket.

Everybody screams in panic. The only difference is in the time it takes the deceased to come to terms with their new status. I have no clue how it works, but the ghost can only exit the casket and roam the cemetery once they've accepted that they're ghosts.

From what I've understood, Clothilde was rather quick. She arrived before me, so I only have her word for it. We once had a young girl who emerged from her urns mere minutes after arriving—but that was a very special case.

Me, I needed something like ten days before accepting my fate. And it wasn't only the whole ghost thing.

When more than a day had gone by and I still wasn't hungry, hadn't needed to take a piss, didn't feel tired—I did realize I was dead. The step from there to accepting you are a ghost isn't terribly steep, especially when you realize you can see your own ghostly body in the dark, that it's all black and white and slightly translucent, and that nothing actually *hurts*, no matter how hard you knock on that lid.

But at least for me, acknowledging I was a ghost wasn't enough to be set free. I also had to acknowledge *why* I was there.

I couldn't remember the exact details of how I died, couldn't remember the last day or two of my life. But I could remember how horribly inadequate I'd been at everything, be it my job or my role as a son, a brother, a friend.

When looking back at my life, I felt nothing but shame.

And I had to come to terms with that, realize why that was, and *want* to fix it, before I was released from my wooden prison.

So when Clothilde first met me, I was already a reformed man.

A man with a mission.

I made it my goal in life—death?—to help as many of our fellow ghosts as possible, by figuring out what they needed to move on to the afterlife. As it turns out, this means I ended up with a rather impressive number of murder cases on my hands and my police training came in handy.

Solving cases while being restricted to the cemetery wasn't easy, but we made do.

"Those ten days in the ground changed me," I say quietly to Clothilde. "They buried a loser but someone at least a little more worthy stepped out of the ground as a ghost."

Clothilde sighs and regards me with a softness I've never seen before. "You're not a loser, Robert. You've done nothing but good since the day you stepped out of your grave. Stop beating yourself up about it. It won't get you anywhere."

I'm about to discard what she says with a scoff but manage to catch myself just in time.

Maybe I should try to listen instead.

Clothilde might look like a teenager, and behave like a rebellious one very frequently, but she's been around for as long as me. If she'd been allowed to live, she would have been fifty-one this year. Older than Evian. Her experiences might have been limited to the cemetery for a large portion of her existence, but it's still experience.

It has still given her maturity.

And I sort of recognize the words as something I would have said to her had our roles been reversed.

And so I nod. Slowly. "You're probably right, Clothilde."

Her eyebrows shoot up and she almost falls through the table as she loses her focus.

"Dwelling on the past won't help me," I say, firmly, mostly trying to convince myself. "I guess I've spent the last thirty years doing penance. Maybe that can be enough?"

I glance at Evian and Doubira on the couch, both focused on what Madame Grand is telling them, Evian taking notes in a paper notebook and Doubira doing the same on his phone.

"I'll try to focus on the present," I say. "We have a unique opportunity here, and I won't be any good to the case if I'm obsessed with mistakes I made in the past. Besides, right now, the past and present seem to be mixing. Maybe I will finally get the chance to right some of my wrongs."

Clothilde smiles but she's starting at me with that laser-look again. "All right, I'll take it. As long as it keeps you from spiraling into depression or something. But don't focus all your hopes on solving this case, you hear me? If we never catch the guys who were behind my death, or that of Gisèle or all the others, you can't let that stop you from moving on. You can't fix everything."

I acknowledge what she's said with a nod but I don't actually answer. I don't think I can promise her that. Stop knocking myself over the head for past mistakes, yes. That, I can do. Really believing that I deserve to move on to the afterlife without righting my greatest wrongs? Sounds a lot more complicated.

"What about you?" I ask her. "Will you accept to move on if they never catch your murderer?"

"We weren't talking about me, Robert." That why-are-you-still-talking-to-me teenager is back. It's her way of changing the subject.

"Will you?" I insist.

"No."

TWENTY-SIX

WITH OUR LITTLE chat, we miss out on most of the interview with Madame Grand but I manage to get a glimpse of Doubira's notes before he puts his phone away. At first, I attempted to read Evian's notes but her handwriting might as well be hieroglyphs for all I know. Doubira's phone offers highly readable text—thank you, technology.

Seems like Gisèle Grand was found dead in a hotel room not far from the City Hall. She died of a heroin overdose sometime during the evening and was discovered by the cleaning lady the next day. Her parents never managed to get their hands on the autopsy report to check if anything other than heroin was detected in her blood. The girl had no history of drugs, hardly ever drank alcohol, and had never touched a cigarette.

At the very bottom of the page, Doubira wrote three names: Gérard de Villenouvelle, Juliette Caju, and Pierre Montbleu.

Doubira turns his phone off and I jump, but not because of the sudden movement.

"I know that name," I say, pointing stupidly at the phone. "Pierre Montbleu. He's the one who sent me to *your* crime scene."

"Well, now. That's certainly interesting." Clothilde jumps down from her perch on the table and we both follow as Doubira and Evian move toward the door. Neither of us particularly wishes to be pulled after Evian every time a door closes behind her.

"He can't possibly still be alive, though," I muse. "The man must have been at least fifty back then."

"So he'd be eighty now." Clothilde shrugs. "He *could* still be alive. But he won't be working anymore."

I shake my head as I slip out the front door and leave Evian and Doubira some space to say goodbye to Madame Grand. "That guy was so overweight he had to use a specially ordered chair in the office. Unless he somehow managed to change his eating habits, there's just no way he's still kicking at eighty."

Once the door is closed, Evian sets a brisk pace down the hallway and down the stairs. "We need to look into those police officers," she says.

"I already checked against Nadine's list," Doubira replies. "And none of them were ever the first officer on the scene. But we already know Gérard de Villenouvelle, of course."

"That we do. We can officially link Gisèle Grand's death with the ongoing case against the man. Which means the girl certainly didn't commit suicide."

"Why didn't you tell her sister as much back there?" Doubira reaches the bottom landing before Evian and holds the door for her as she rushes through.

"A day or week more or less won't make a difference now. I'd much prefer to have something more definite and certain before getting her hopes up."

"Should we ask for an exhumation?"

They've already reached the car and Evian has the door open but she stops to meet Doubira's gaze over the roof of the small rental. "We need the family's consent to do an exhumation. Which would mean telling Madame Grand everything we know. I don't expect the body to tell us much—except possibly officially link Monsieur de Villenouvelle to the crime—so I vote we use the information we got from Madame Grand and explore all the other avenues first."

"Like looking into Madame Caju and Monsieur Montbleu?"

"Yes, like that." Evian taps the car roof twice with her palm then gets into the car.

Clothilde and I are quick to get into the back seat. When Evian has slammed the door shut and starts the car, Clothilde leans forward and says straight into Evian's ear, "You should start with Monsieur Montbleu. He'll get you your link to Robert Villemur."

Evian backs out of her parking space and takes a right—straight into rush hour traffic. "I'd like to start with Pierre Montbleu," she says.

"Sure," Doubira says lightly. "I'll send the name to Nadine and ask her to look into it."

Clothilde leans back in her seat and we share a look.

"That's bloody impressive—and useful," I say.

Clothilde chuckles evilly. If she was an upset teenager in my home, I'd be worried. "We're going to get these guys," she says. "Just wait and see."

TWENTY-SEVEN

Nadine Tulle is clearly a miracle worker. When we walk into her tiny office an hour and a half later—that traffic was *lethal*—she has already done all the research Doubira asked her for.

"I can't stay long," Tulle says in lieu of greeting. "I wanted to wait until you got back to do the handover, but in ten minutes I'm on the metro on my way home."

"Of course," Evian says, the most genuine smile I've seen from her yet gracing her otherwise rather stern features. "Give us the highlights and the files and you can be on your way."

A slight tension that I hadn't even realized was there goes out of Tulle's shoulders. She wants in on working with Evian but not at any price. Clearly, her personal life is important to her.

"Last things first," Tulle says and hands over a tiny stick-like thing to Doubira. "Pierre Montbleu was Robert Villemur's boss. Sort of."

He was? Ironically, this is news to me. Because, yes, I was stupid enough to follow the orders of someone who—as far as I knew—*wasn't* my boss.

"Sort of?" Evian asks. She is leaning against the window-sill. Tulle has her own office but it's *tiny*. There's barely enough room for a desk and a chair so with the door closed and two extra people—not to mention two ghosts—the space feels very crowded. I get the feeling Evian prefers to be close to the window to get the impression of space.

"Villemur worked for a woman named Durand, who worked for a man called Parayre, who had strong links with Montbleu."

"A bit far-fetched if we're looking at corrupt cops," Evian muses. "Too many middle men. But it *is* a link."

Tulle nods, making her blond braid jump against her chest. "Montbleu died almost twenty years ago—"

"A shame he didn't come through our cemetery," Clothilde comments lightly.

"—Durand is alive but in a nursing home and suffering from Alzheimer's, and Parayre is still alive and kicking, working as a consultant for the police here in Toulouse."

I shake my head. "I've never heard of Parayre or Durand. I took my orders directly from Montbleu because he promised me an easy promotion. I'm only now realizing that he actually *could* do that. Not sure if that makes me any less stupid. Still." I shake out of my irrelevant thoughts and turn to speak clearly to Evian. "There's no point in looking into the elderly middle men."

Evian doesn't say anything but signs for Tulle to continue her report.

"I've added location to all the deaths you had me search earlier. There's a little bit of everything but the number of hotels *is* surprisingly high."

"Those will be the ones we look into first," Evian says to Doubira, who nods.

"I've done some cross-referencing," Tulle says. She grabs her braid and throws it over her shoulder. That seems to be a nervous tic. "If any of the police officers had any kind of hierarchical link with Villemur or de Villenouvelle, the info is in the file. I've mentioned if the officer was located elsewhere than Toulouse, as this might mean it's less likely they had a link with the people we're after. Whenever possible, I've also noted if the officer was known for being easily influenced."

Three pairs of eyebrows shoot up, with only Clothilde not finding this information particularly surprising. "How did you get hold of *that* information?" Evian asks.

Tulle purses her lips as she looks from Evian to Doubira, and back again at Evian. "You may not want to know that. There's a reason I'm giving you the information on a USB drive and not sent over the network. I've been working exclusively on the drive—so there's only one other copy and I have that in my pocket—and I may have…improvised somewhat on certain aspects of my search."

Evian turns her head to look out the window for a moment, then takes a deep breath. "Ignorance is bliss, isn't that so?"

Tulle grabs her braid and brings it back to the front. I don't know the woman well enough to read her yet but I think she realizes she took a great risk by putting highly confidential information in the file. And she also knows it will be helpful, so she did it anyway.

Evian flips what is apparently called a USB drive over in her hand. "Should I read this on my computer here at the station?"

The flinch is small but it's there. "At home would be better. Preferably while you're not connected to the internet."

Doubira eyes the tiny little object in Evian's hand that apparently holds so many secrets. "Isn't that a little extreme?"

"Better safe than sorry." Tulle gives her braid one last tug and nods to Evian. "I have to go. Please let me know if there's anything else I can do for you. In any case, I'll try to find the time to continue mining the data tomorrow."

"Thank you, Nadine," Evian says. Her eyes are soft as she watches the smaller woman leave. When the door closes behind her, she turns her gaze on Doubira. "Well, Malik, I think it's time we called it a day, too. I'd invite you home to look at the files with me but I don't think we're quite there in our relationship yet."

Doubira breaks out in a huge smile, flashing all his perfectly white teeth. "That's okay. I'll watch one episode of something stupid and dive right into bed. I'm exhausted. I'll take the files tomorrow night if you want."

"That sounds great." The softness has stayed with Evian. It's like her body has decided that the work day is indeed over and the hardness she imposes on it is letting go.

"You did great today, Doubira," she says as he exits the office.

He acknowledges the compliment with a tip of his imaginary hat, and then he's gone.

Evian stays, leaning against the windowsill. My little finger tingles as she touches the bones in her pocket, stroking them if I'm not mistaken. She seems pensive. And tired.

I lean in and speak softly in her ear. "You did good, too."

TWENTY-EIGHT

EMELINE BREATHES OUT a heartfelt sigh as she pulls open the front door of her building. Even at this hour of the night there was traffic. She might need to ask for a bike in lieu of a rental car—it would allow her to get around faster.

It's been a long day and she's exhausted. To the point of hesitating in front of the elevator. Usually, she takes the stairs. It's just two floors, it's exercise, and it means she doesn't have to stand in a moving box as if that's a natural place for a human to hang out.

Still. Tonight it's almost tempting.

Almost.

Emeline takes one step toward the staircase then stops as someone opens the front door and a whoosh of chill evening air flows over her.

It's her neighbor. Amina. With the exuberant, curly hair and sparkling green eyes.

"Hey there, neighbor!" she says with a huge smile. She lets the front door slide shut behind her and walks—at a normal pace and not skipping or running—across the lobby to press the elevator button.

Her smile is as brilliant as Emeline remembers but her eyes are tired. She wouldn't qualify her posture as a slouch, exactly, but it's definitely more subdued than the other day.

"Long day at work?" Emeline asks. She's still standing in the middle of the lobby, halfway to the staircase.

Amina rolls her eyes and groans. "The longest! I had this client who was *such* a pain in the ass, and then he decided to complain to management. Which went fine, by the way, my boss isn't about to let idiots like that mess with her staff, but it took almost forty-five minutes, so all my *other* clients were annoyed by the delay. And now I'm coming home almost an hour later than usual."

The elevator doors slide open and Amina steps in.

Emeline follows. "What kind of job do you do?" She presses the button for the second floor and as she leans close to Amina she notices a smell of coconut. It's relaxing.

"Oh, on Wednesdays I'm a masseuse. The salon is just two metro stops away and my boss is really cool. So it's great." That huge smile again. It seems like even exhausted, this woman exudes energy and joy.

"On Wednesdays?"

The elevator comes to a stop and the doors slide open. Amina walks out. "I have three different jobs," she says lightly. "Never

135

could decide what I wanted to do with my life. So I'm doing all of it."

Emeline stares at her neighbor in surprise. Then realizes she's standing in the elevator when she should be getting out. And that the ride hadn't freaked her out in the least. Apparently exhaustion is good for something.

She's about to ask Amina what her other two jobs are, but the woman beats her to it.

"So what do you do?" She looks Emeline up and down as they walk side by side down the corridor. "Something tiring with long hours, apparently."

"I'm a police officer," Emeline answers. She tries to gauge Amina's reaction out of the corner of her eye. Not everyone likes the police.

But Amina gives Emeline a quick once-over. "Yeah, that fits."

Emeline can't help but chuckle. "I don't think that's a compliment."

"Maybe you *should* think so." Amina comes to a stop in front of her door but makes no sign of getting her keys. "Why would you assume that looking like you're a police officer is a bad thing? Do you associate the police with being unjust? Oppressors? Or is it a femininity thing? Why shouldn't a female police officer be sexy? There are other forms of femininity than huge boobs and skirts."

Emeline stands there gaping for a moment. She's not getting her keys either, and her arms are hanging limp by her sides as she tries to take in the tirade her neighbor threw at her.

"Well." She shakes her head, trying to get some last mileage out of her brain before it shuts down for good for the night. "I guess I'm used to people not being particularly open to the police being human, too. It's often easier to look at us as 'other.' And I'm not going to go into the whole femininity thing at this time of night. My brain's not up for it."

"Which means I'm right. You think a woman needs a dress or a skirt to qualify as sexy or feminine."

Emeline chuckles and shakes her head. She finally remembers which pocket her house keys are in and takes a step toward her own door to open it. "Too late, Amina. Try me again some other time."

The tiredness is still apparent in Amina's eyes, but her smile is genuine and playful. "I will."

They both unlock their doors and Emeline gives a small nod.

"Wait!" Amina takes one step into Emeline's apartment to stop her from closing the door. "You haven't told me *your* name."

"It's Emeline." She wonders if she should invite the woman in now that she's halfway there anyway, but she really is too tired.

And Amina doesn't seem to have been fishing for an invitation because she steps away immediately. Still smiling. "That suits you, too."

When she's finally in her own living room, sitting in the silence with an empty bowl of cereal on the coffee table and her current mystery novel abandoned because it took too much effort to read, she pulls out the two finger bones from her pocket.

She's been carrying them around all day, like some sort of talisman of her motivation for solving this case. At least that's what she thinks it is. For some reason, she cannot bear the thought of parting with them, as weird as that sounds.

The gut feeling that has helped her so often in the past is particularly strong on this case—and it's linked to the bones.

Perhaps Clothilde and Robert are somehow with her as she searches for answers on their behalf.

Emeline starts to scoff at her own thought but doesn't even finish as she rolls the bones over in her hand.

Bones won't help her solve the case. Hard work will do that. Bones won't help her keep her focus. It's a given she will stay focused until she either finds the killers or has tried absolutely everything. That's just how she's wired.

But she's not getting rid of the bones.

Might as well accept it.

And she should find a safer and more discreet means of transportation than her jacket pocket. She doesn't want to lose them if she gets hot and throws her jacket over her arm.

Even more importantly, she doesn't want anyone else to see them and realize she stole pieces of the victims of her current serial killer case.

That might not go over so well.

She needs to keep them safe and keep them hidden.

She turns them over in her hand a couple of times. They're really not very big. She could sew them into the lining of a piece of clothing and nobody would be the wiser. Except she doesn't have a piece of clothing that she wears every single day. She might be able to fit them into her wallet somehow but this actually increases the chances of discovery.

She could make them into a necklace. Or a bracelet. Anyone who knows her will know that a necklace is not normal—but she can pull off a wrist bracelet.

So despite the hour, she sets to work. The previous tenant left behind a box of threads, buttons, and other colorful stuff, and Emeline finds everything she needs. She doesn't try to do anything fancy, she simply places the bones on a thick piece of thread, and then uses thinner colorful threads to wrap them to the central piece, round and round until they're secured tightly, and in no danger of slipping from their cocoon. Less than an hour later, she has a bracelet which will go twice around her wrist, with two sections that are thicker than the rest that will rest against each other.

Suddenly, she realizes she hasn't even attempted to look at the file that Nadine Tulle gave her earlier. She was too tired, and then decided what little energy she had left should be spent making necromancer jewelry.

She holds up the bracelet to frown at it. "What *is* it with you guys? What the hell is going on?" Shaking her head, she places the bracelet on the kitchen counter. "I'm not going to figure this out tonight. But one thing is certain: you're staying out here."

Then she goes to her room, her comfortable bed calling to her.

She closes the door firmly behind her.

TWENTY-NINE

THE NEXT MORNING we ride into the police station on Evian's wrist—not our ghostly forms, of course, but our earthly remains. My right little finger tingles slightly with every movement, as the threads tighten around the bone but I'm sure it's a feeling I'll get used to.

Evian has decided to leave the rental car at home today and walked the kilometer between her apartment and the station. I think she quite enjoyed the walk, and so did Clothilde and I. It allowed us to take our time in observing the changes of the city, and the people around us in general.

As Evian pushes through the revolving doors into the police station at nine o'clock sharp—a couple of weird seconds there when we are forced to squeeze into the small space with her—she is greeted by three people loitering at the reception desk. A woman in her late forties who is out of uniform but clearly police, with short dark hair and brown eyes that don't seem to miss much. One black man with salt-and-pepper hair and a matching mustache who must be close to two meters tall. He towers over the other two by at least a head. I'd say he's in his fifties but this estimation is based solely on the color of his hair. The last man looks Spanish, with tanned skin and dark hair and eyes. Probably closing in on forty.

"Emeline Evian?" the woman asks as Evian is about to walk past them toward her office.

Now she stops, pulls her shoulders back and give all three of them a once-over before replying. "Who's asking?" She's not exactly hostile but she seems to have decided they're not here to chat about the weather.

I agree with her assessment.

Clothilde is already in the middle of the group, studying them up close. "You know any of these clowns?"

"How would I? These people were in diapers or at best in high school when I worked here. They might look older than me, but they're actually not, you know."

"Hmm." She steps up on an imaginary support to get close enough to study the tall guy's features—from less than a hand's breadth away. I'm glad nobody can see her because in real life her behavior might have warranted a trip to the doctor. "This guy doesn't really look at ease."

I'm curious what she means but decide not to say anything. I don't want to miss what they're saying to Evian.

"I'm Sophie Spangero," the woman says, the annoyance in her voice clearly betraying that she doesn't usually require an introduction. "Head of the region's Judicial Police."

141

My eyebrows shoot up. She might have been right in expecting to be recognized. The Toulouse PJ must answer to the regional PJ, who in turn answers to the guys at 36, Quai des Orfèvres in Paris. I'm not sure who decided to invite Evian to come down here from Paris to investigate, but it must not have been this woman since Evian doesn't seem to know her.

Spangero must be quite a few steps above Evian in the police pecking order but that doesn't seem to scare Evian.

"This is Nouh Diome," Spangero continues, indicating the tall man. "Head of the Toulouse PJ."

Diome nods his head gravely at Evian. "We are acquainted," he says in a voice so deep I'm wondering if he has built-in bass speakers in his pockets. "I am the one who asked Captain Evian to come to Toulouse, after all."

Well, that's one question answered. And his use of Evian's official title is interesting.

Spangero indicates the last man. "And Diego Gonzales, my right-hand man."

Evian shakes hands with everybody. I'm proud to see her attitude in the face of a group of people who all outrank her. She's not going to scrape and bow just because they expect her to.

Spangero asks Evian to follow them to Diome's office, and since this group is not one for chit-chatting, I take the opportunity to talk to Clothilde again.

"What made you say Diome wasn't at ease?"

While I'm walking a few steps behind the group, Clothilde is still right up in their faces, studying their facial expressions and body movements. She's gone straight through Spangero two times already but the woman has made no sign of noticing.

"His breathing was uneven," Clothilde answers absently as she stares intently at Gonzales's neck. "He hid it well, but he seemed really nervous. Kept swallowing and sweat was forming at his temples."

She points at Spangero, who is walking a couple of steps ahead of everyone else, her low heels clacking angrily against the tiled floor. "She's pissed off."

I chuckle. "Even I can tell that much."

"Yeah, but she's even more angry than she's letting on, I think. Her pulse is off the roof and her breathing really, really short."

I glance over at Evian, wondering if I should somehow warn her, only to discover that her eyes are on the woman stalking along ahead of her, making an assessment. She might have picked up on the clues all by herself, but I'm guessing Clothilde's observations are also helping.

Clothilde chews on her lip, her face still way too close to Gonzales's for comfort. "This guy, I can't figure out," she says. "I get the feeling he wants to please his boss, but he keeps sending worried glances at the tall dude. There's tension here and this guy doesn't like it."

As we walk into Diome's office, Doubira comes out of the men's room down the hallway. When he sees Evian, he takes a step toward her but Evian gives a slight shake of her head and he stops.

Inside the office, Evian closes the door behind her without being told.

Spangero sits down behind the desk, in Diome's chair, and silently invites everybody else to take a seat in the visitors' chairs across from her.

Except there are only two chairs.

Evian solves the problem by standing at parade rest next to the door. "What did you want to talk to me about that had you coming all the way from Bordeaux?"

Spangero frowns up at Evian, probably regretting her choice to sit down. "I did not come here for you. I have meetings here all afternoon, which were set up long before you set foot in Toulouse."

An awful lot of justification for a big boss to give to someone so far below her own station.

"I did, however, hear about the work you're doing, and, frankly, I am worried."

Clothilde sidles up to me where I'm standing in the far corner in order to cause as little distraction as possible for Evian, and whispers, "She *should* be worried, right? With all the sloppy police work that her people have been doing for so long?"

"Yes. But if she's as angry as you say, and it seems to be directed at Evian, that might not be the reason she's upset. I hope Evian will let her explain and not jump to any conclusions."

Evian does just that, and doesn't say a word.

After a few seconds of silence, Spangero continues. "You were brought to Toulouse to look into the deaths of two young women. Now I learn that you've requested the exhumation of not two, but *thirty-eight*, women and that you're bringing the work of colleagues into question."

"I *was* brought down here to look into two deaths," Evian replies calmly. "We quickly discovered that they were indeed murders and not suicides, as had first been concluded. It didn't take much work to see there was a pattern, which is why we requested the other exhumations. Four of those were obvious matches because of the DNA found on the victims. The rest are most likely linked, too, it's just going to be more difficult to prove."

The anger in Spangero's eyes is impossible to miss now. "You were asked to look into *two* deaths."

"I was given a case, and I worked it like I would any other. When I see a pattern, I've been trained to look into it. If we have a suspected serial killer, it's our duty to go after him, not look the other way."

"You're not looking for a serial killer, Evian. You're trying to make the Toulouse police look bad."

Evian raises a lazy eyebrow. "What makes you say that?"

"I know you've been looking into who worked on the cases you've been investigating. I know you think only you Parisians know how to work a murder case. You're trying to make us look bad."

Evian sighs. "If I make you look bad, it's going to be because you didn't do your jobs. If the officers who worked those cases really did do their best, then that's what it will say in my report."

Spangero slams a hand on the desk, making a dying plant on the other end jump and shake its leaves. "I do not want a report on how the Toulouse police does their work! We asked you to look into those two specific cases, and that's all. You *do* know how to follow orders, Evian?"

Jaw working, Evian takes a few seconds to reply. She's still at parade rest, which means her hands are hidden from the rest of the room, but I can see them clenching and unclenching.

"Of course I can," she finally replies, her voice flat. "You will have the report on your desk within the week. It *will* include information on the four extra girls who we know are linked to the case, though. I cannot remove that knowledge now."

She takes a calming breath, steeling herself. "May I make one request, though? We found the remains of a police officer who worked here thirty years ago, one Robert Villemur. He was in an unmarked grave in a small cemetery on the outskirts of Toulouse. Will you allow me to look into his case? He was clearly murdered and it's generally not a good idea to let the public think they can get away with such action against the police."

As Spangero takes her time replying, her eyes never blinking as she stares down Evian, the two other men in the room are as immobile and silent as they have been throughout the meeting. Gonzales's eyes jump back and forth between the two women, clearly not wanting to miss anything, while Diome's gaze hasn't left that poor plant on his desk since he sat down in his own visitors' chair. He's listening to every word but isn't letting any of his thoughts or emotions show.

"You can look into the case of this Villemur," Spangero says finally. "But I'm the first to see the report. It will only be shown to the public if it puts the Toulouse police in a good light. This de Villenouvelle business is bad enough, we don't need to add anything else to it."

Evian nods curtly. "I can live with that."

"I didn't ask if you could live with it," Spangero says. "I gave you an order and I expect you to follow it. And once this case is closed, I want you on the first flight back to Paris."

THIRTY

SOME SORT OF silent communication must have taken place between Diome and Evian while I wasn't looking. When the meeting ends, Evian does a quick trip to the restroom—stalls not going all the way to the ceiling, luckily, so we can wait outside—and then goes right back to Diome's office.

He's the only one there and he's recovered his chair. He's using a small water bottle to water his plant but I'm not convinced it's going to do much good.

"Close the door, please, Emeline," he rumbles in that deep voice but Evian has already clicked the door shut behind her.

This time she sits in one of the visitors' chairs and her stance is more relaxed. "What happened?"

Diome sighs and leans back in his chair so it creaks while he steeples his fingers over his flat belly. "This conversation is off the record, yes? If anyone asks, we are talking about how to keep a plant alive in an office with no direct sunlight."

"Your plant will be dead in two weeks," Evian says.

Clothilde cackles and jumps up to perch on Diome's desk, feet dangling.

"Right," Diome says. "So, as you see, this conversation about my plant really did take place here today."

"What's got Spangero's knickers in a twist?"

"I do not know, exactly." Diome rolls his shoulders as if trying to work a kink out. "I received a phone call in the late afternoon yesterday, saying she would be here very early to talk to me. She also said to make sure you would be here but without giving you forewarning."

"Was she really planning on coming here, or did she make that up?"

"From what I understand, she was scheduled to come, but only this afternoon. She made the journey last night instead of this morning."

Evian runs a hand over the new bracelet, making my little finger tingle. "I guess that could explain the crappy mood, if she hasn't had any sleep."

Diome shakes his head. "The mood was the same yesterday." He has a way of pronouncing every word exactly, and with great care, which, mixed with his deep voice, makes him sound poised and calm and thoughtful. It makes him feel trustworthy—which is a feeling I'm not entirely sure I should trust.

"So, which part of my investigation made alarm bells go off on her end, do you think?" Evian asks.

"You tell me, Emeline. You tell me. I have not heard a lot of details of the work you have done here. I have kept my distance, as we discussed before your arrival, so that I would not influence you or make it too clear who had wanted you to come to Toulouse in the first place."

"Spangero knows."

"Yes, but not many others. Anyone above my paygrade will know, but nobody below it. At least, they will not have learned it from me."

Evian narrows her eyes. "So you're telling me that if I meet someone here who knows you're the one who requested my presence, they will have gotten the information elsewhere?"

"Yes. Quite so. Do you know of someone who knows?"

Clothilde is following the conversation like a tennis match, her head going back and forth, back and forth. I appreciate that she's staying quiet so we can follow the conversation. I'm also kind of surprised at how seriously she's taking all this. I'm used to a moody teenager who doesn't like to take things seriously, who lets herself get distracted by anything. But since the moment Evian showed up in our cemetery to exhume her, she has been one hundred percent focused on the case.

Guess all she needed was proper motivation.

"I haven't really talked to that many people around here yet," Evian replies to Diome. "But I'll keep my ears open if the subject comes up."

"And how is Malik Doubira working out as a partner?"

Evian smiles, the first genuine one of the day. "He seems great. Thank you for assigning him to me."

Diome nods gravely. "I believe he has great potential. Let me know if you need anything or anybody else, yes?"

"I've already contracted the help of Nadine Tulle for research," Evian says. "I was planning on perhaps including more people, but now I think we'll stay with a restricted group." She runs a hand through her short hair, making a few strands above her left ear stand up. "In any case, I guess I'll mostly be focusing on figuring out what happened to Robert Villemur."

The chair creaks as Diome leans forward to place his folded hands on the desk. "Yes. Let us follow orders. There may still be ways to discover some things."

Maybe I should have seen it coming, but I'm genuinely floored by the implications of what he's saying. He really did expect Evian to find something suspicious within the ranks of the police force in Toulouse. He knew the deaths of Lise and Manon, who were both buried in our cemetery before we left, were not isolated cases.

He probably also knew that someone would try to put a stop to it at some point. I just hope he'll be looking into it on his end, as well. Evian will be forced to keep her focus where the big boss ordered her to keep it.

"There's a definite link between Villemur and some of the murdered girls," Evian tells Diome. "But maybe I'll keep that link less obvious in my reports from now on."

"Yes," Diome agrees in his deep rumble. "That might be best. In any case, I am also curious about what happened to this man. How did a police officer's disappearance not result in more consequences?"

Evian touches the bracelet again. "I'm curious about him, too. Having him as a first step suits me just fine." She gets up from the chair and levels Diome with a serious look. "I expect you to make sure I'll be allowed to make the steps that come after."

Diome gets up and shakes her hand before she exits the office. "I will do my best."

THIRTY-ONE

"Okay, what just happened in there?" Clothilde asks me as we follow Evian through the police station. "Is that Spangero woman our bad guy?"

"That scene certainly didn't make her look too good," I reply. "But let's not jump to conclusions yet. She might have other motivations for stopping Evian than covering for a murderer."

Clothilde studies me, a tiny frown marring her forehead. "What other motivations could she have? She outright forbade Evian from looking into the deaths of more young women. She'll only let the public know about *you* if it makes the police look good."

151

"And that's the point that makes it at least *possible* that she doesn't have any nefarious intentions. She's head of the Judicial Police of the entire region. She needs us to look good. Finding out there's been a serial killer on the loose for over thirty years does *not* make us look good."

Clothilde ponders my words as we stroll down an empty corridor with closed doors every three meters. The only light comes from fluorescent bulbs overhead, and had Clothilde still been alive it would probably have made her look pale and ghostly. That's certainly the effect it has on Evian.

"Or she's our bad guy," Clothilde says, making me think of a grumpy teenager for the first time in quite a while.

So I smile at her, happy to recognize my friend even if it's not particularly flattering. "She could be," I agree. "And we'll keep it in mind. But before we can start throwing out accusations—or rather, have Evian throw out accusations—we need proof."

Clothilde scoffs but I'm sure she's taken my warning to heart. She's a smart girl, after all.

Although I'm trying to stop Clothilde from making accusations, my mind is moving in much the same direction as hers, just with more warnings and stop signals along the way.

In the entire Judicial Police, Spangero has only one person above her, the Judicial Police Chief of Staff in Paris. If someone of her caliber changed her schedule to come to Toulouse from Bordeaux, basically in the middle of the night, to make sure Evian didn't poke at things she didn't want poked, it means important forces are in play.

There is no doubt that the woman was angry. The question is why. Is it anger that Evian risks discovering something that will make Spangero look bad? Does Spangero indeed have some connection with de Villenouvelle or whoever else was in league with the man for all the killings?

Or was her anger based in fear? It could be fear of losing her position, or fear for herself. Someone *could* be threatening her.

"I'd love to have some info on Spangero's family situation," I say out loud, half to myself and half to Evian, to plant a little seed.

"Why? Is she your type?" Clothilde's smile is huge and impish. "You never did tell me what you look for in a woman. Is powerful and angry your thing? I'm not sure the whole alive/ghost thing is worth pursuing."

I can't help but crack a smile. "Ha ha. Very funny. I was just wondering if she has some vulnerabilities that could be exploited."

Clothilde stops in her tracks, her eyes wide. "You want us to blackmail the woman?"

Evian arrives at her desk and as she sits down, she huffs a laugh.

It's eerie how sensitive this woman is. It's like she's following our conversation word for word. I wonder how she's arguing the logic in her own head. Does she think she's hearing voices? Is she taking our dialogue for her own thoughts?

Evian starts up the computer at her desk and exchanges a few words on the weather with the grandmotherly woman at the next desk over. She doesn't seem overly upset about the encounter with Spangero—but I suspect she's very good at hiding her feelings and is probably mulling everything over much the way I'm doing.

"Really?" Clothilde says as she jumps up to perch on the elderly officer's desk. "We're going to look for ways to put pressure on the big boss?"

"No," I tell her. "That's not what I meant. And I certainly hope it's not what Evian has in mind, especially if she's working on the office computer on the police network." I'm far from being up to speed on modern technology, but I've picked up enough during overheard conversations in the cemetery and passing comments over the last few days to know that anything can be monitored.

Always assume someone's watching.

"I meant that I'd like to know if she has some vulnerability that *someone else* could exploit."

"Like what?"

"Like a family member that's being threatened. Or someone who will get the job he wants or get into the school she's dreamed of for years, so long as Spangero does as she's told." I consider my own words, and add, "Although I hope it's not any of those last two, because that would be frankly disappointing from someone of her caliber and position."

Clothilde swings her feet back and forth, her hands under her thighs. It's like being back in the cemetery, where she always sat like this on her own tombstone. "Oh, okay," she says, losing interest now that *we're* not the ones doing the blackmailing. She turns to look at the officer on whose desk she's squatting, squinting at whatever is on the woman's computer screen.

I take up position behind Evian and watch as she opens a window with Doubira's name and picture at the top.

Could you find us a decent restaurant for lunch? she writes.

Sure, Doubira replies almost immediately. **Any special requests?**

I like this guy. He realized something was going on this morning but doesn't ask about it outright. And now he's wondering if Evian wants to eat in a place with lots of police officers or in a place without them.

We'll be visiting Villemur's brother or sister, Evian types. **Find something close to wherever they live.**

My heart jumps in my throat at the idea of seeing my brother or my sister again but I force myself to focus. Evian wants to see them to learn more about me. No matter which brother we're talking about, my sister is the better bet with that goal in mind.

"Go for the sister," I say into Evian's ear just as Doubira's next message pops up.

They're in different parts of the city, he writes. **No preference between the two?**

Maybe go with the sister first, Evian types. Then adds to herself, "Women are more perceptive."

Close enough to the truth. Seems like she *is* arguing that whatever I tell her is common sense and her own subconscious.

Do you want us to go see Nadine before we leave?

Evian licks her lips. Glances at her watch. It's only ten. **I think we should try to fit the interview in before lunch**, she replies after some rumination. **Make sure Tulle will be here late this afternoon and we'll see her then.**

She doesn't want to see the efficient Tulle too soon. She hopes the woman will find some interesting information before she has to officially take her off the case. Off the case of the dead young women, anyway.

I'm kind of curious about what the research whiz will be able to find on my history.

A new message pops up from Doubira. **Got Caroline Sanchez's (the sister) address. It's across town. Do you want me to call ahead?**

Make a call pretending to sell something, Evian types. **I don't want to lose too much time but I'd rather she didn't have time to prepare for our arrival.**

What kind of preparation is she expecting? She's not suspecting my *sister* of having had anything to do with my death, surely?

Are we taking your car? Doubira asks.

We're taking the metro, Evian replies and she actually growls at the computer, making the lady at the next desk look over in surprise. "If I have my way, I'll never drive in this city again."

THIRTY-TWO

CAROLINE SANCHEZ LIVES in a ground floor apartment in an old but well-maintained building at the very end of a cul-de-sac in a calm and sleepy neighborhood in the north part of Toulouse. It takes Emeline and Malik forty minutes to get there from the police station—twenty-five minutes of metro and fifteen minutes on foot.

It might have taken the same time in a car but at least now Emeline isn't annoyed and angry at life in general. She's had the time to ponder the case in peace while they were crammed into the very back of the last car of the metro, and she took the opportunity to chat with her colleague during their walk. They didn't talk about the case, partly because Emeline has always been a little paranoid about talking about cases out in public, but mainly because she wants to get to know the man who's working this case with her.

Malik is the fourth of five kids and grew up in one of the more mixed neighborhoods of the city. During his childhood his family was far from poor—his father worked as a high school teacher and his mother a nanny—but he had classmates who were much better off than him financially. Emeline gets the feeling he probably lived through some injustices because of his social standing though he doesn't say it outright. It was probably part of his motivation for his chosen career path, though.

Malik asks some questions but Emeline mostly avoids answering anything too personal. She likes getting to know her colleagues but she'll only share her own secrets with people she trusts completely.

Having Malik answer questions helps to move him toward that trust.

"There's a gymnasium not far from here," Malik says, waving a hand to their left, indicating some spot behind a group of small but pretty houses. "We sometimes have games there."

Emeline lets her eyes run up and down Malik's tall body. "Basket?"

Malik flashes that huge grin of his, making him look like he should be in class in the high school they passed before entering the cul-de-sac. "Basket. It's the only sport worth playing."

They reach the gate at the end of the street and Emeline presses the down arrow on the intercom, searching for Sanchez's name. "The *only* sport?" she says with a laugh. "That's a risky claim so far into rugby-land."

Malik scoffs good-naturedly. "Rugby is just brute force. There's no finesse, no art."

"Care to take that up with Diome?" Emeline seems to remember hearing that he played professionally in his youth—not surprising, considering his size.

"Nah. I don't want to hurt his feelings or anything."

"Good plan."

A faint voice comes out of the intercom, probably asking who's there.

"Captain Evian and Lieutenant Doubira of the Judicial Police, Madame," Emeline says loudly into the microphone. "We'd like to come in and talk to you for a moment."

No more sounds come out of the intercom but after a few seconds the smaller of the two gates clicks open.

"Do we know where we're going?" Emeline asks Malik.

He shrugs and pushes through the gate, holding it for her to follow. "She's on the ground floor, apartment number four. Shouldn't be too complicated."

Two minutes later, they find apartment number four at the end of a brightly lit hallway, where a woman is waiting for them with the door cracked open. She looks to be in her sixties, with hair such a beautiful brown color Emeline suspects she dyes it, and quite a few wrinkles marking her face—but more from smiling than frowning. Her eyes are blue and alert as she assesses Emeline and Malik.

Emeline doesn't miss the fact that she stays well inside of the door and can easily slam it shut in less than a second.

"Caroline Sanchez?" Emeline asks. "I'm Captain Evian and this is Lieutenant Doubira." She holds out her hand and after only a slight hesitation, Madame Sanchez exits her apartment far enough to shake it.

"What brings you here, Madame?" The woman glances at the IDs Emeline and Doubira show, clearly knowing what to look for and identifying Emeline as the senior officer in the pair.

"We'd like to talk to you about your brother," Emeline says. "Robert Villemur, that is," she adds as she remembers the woman has three, and two of them still alive.

The surprise on the woman's face isn't faked. She seems to forget to breathe for a moment as her mouth falls open, and her hand, which was stretched out in front of her after shaking Malik's hand, drops to her side.

"Robert? But..." She looks from Emeline to Malik and back again. Then down the hallway behind them, as if expecting someone to jump out and yell surprise. And not a good surprise. "What— He never— What?"

"Would you mind if we come in?" Emeline says, keeping her tone gentle.

"Yes. Yes, of course." Madame Sanchez steps back and lets the front door slide open. She gestures. "Come in. Why don't you step into the kitchen and I'll make some tea or coffee."

Emeline appreciates how the woman recovers so quickly. And she's very happy at not having to drink coffee. "I'd love a cup of tea, Madame," she says. "But I suspect my colleague will take you up on the offer of coffee."

They move into a modern kitchen in white and several shades of gray. The small table can seat four, and Emeline and Malik take seats on the same side to sit opposite Robert Villemur's sister. While their hostess prepares their drinks, Emeline studies the pictures framed on the wall and attached by magnets to the fridge.

Madame Sanchez must be a grandmother. There are pictures of at least five different kids below the age of six and several drawings for "Mamie." Some pictures also contain adults who might be in their mid-thirties, and they definitely share some DNA with the woman preparing coffee.

She wonders if any of them remember their uncle.

Madame Sanchez places a steaming cup in front of Emeline, another one for Malik, and a third one for herself. "Tell me about Robert."

Emeline takes a deep breath. "We found where they buried his body."

THIRTY-THREE

CAROLINE'S APARTMENT IS great. It suits her.

When I was alive, she and her family were squeezed into a three-bedroom apartment in one of the city's more seedy neighborhoods, worrying about the school they were going to send their kids to and whether or not it was safe for Caroline to go out alone at night.

I know it's thirty years later and that she should, by all rights, have manged to get out of that hellhole by now, but I'm still very happy that she did.

My sister lives in a safe and calm street. She has four bedrooms, and two of them are clearly mostly unused guest rooms. She's still married, if the ring on her finger is anything to go by.

She has at least five grandchildren. And…I go so far as to walking through Doubira to get to some of the pictures. That dark-haired man with the beginnings of a pot-belly—that must be Mathieu. He still has the same lop-sided smile, and has passed it on to his sons. Three of them! And the lean man with a shaved head and about five days' worth of blond beard? Definitely Antoine. I can't believe I recognize him when I haven't seen him since he was two. Soulful, blue eyes, impossible to miss.

But in two of these pictures, I see an entire family of four. And I don't recognize any of them, except that there's a definite Villemur family resemblance. From the mother.

Did Caroline have a third child after my death?

Somehow this makes me even more sad than having missed out on everybody growing up.

When Caroline asks Evian for news about me, I sit down on the empty chair next to my sister. Clothilde has found a kitchen counter to perch on and she's studying my sister closely.

I touch a hand to Caroline's—I can't feel her and she can't feel me, but I need to do it anyway. My sister. Who's even older than my mother was when I passed away. Before I can stop them, my fingers lift to trace the wrinkles at her eyes and the sagging skin on her jaw.

A tear starts to form in her eye, so I stop. Looks like she's at least a little sensitive.

"I didn't really believe he was alive," she says to Evian in a small voice. She lowers her beautiful blue eyes to her cup, where her spotted hands are curled around it for heat. "I think it's good to finally know," she adds after a moment's thought. "I think."

Evian nods. "It usually is better to know. Especially after this long."

"Do you know if he died when he disappeared?"

163

"It seems likely," Evian replies. "It was too long ago for the coroner to be able to tell when he died to within more than a year or two. But he's been dead for approximately thirty years, and the location he was found in seems to indicate that he disappeared because he died."

"Where did you find him?"

Doubira speaks up for the first time since we got here. "He was illegally buried in an unmarked grave in a cemetery in one of the villages outside of Toulouse."

Caroline's eyebrows shoot up and her hands twitch around her cup. "*Illegally* buried in an *unmarked* grave? How is that even possible?"

"That's part of what we'll be looking into, Madame," Doubira says smoothly. "All I can say is that his casket was right next to another one that we exhumed, so we happened upon it while digging."

"You *happened* upon his casket while digging up someone else." She's repeating what she's being told in order to try to make sense of it. She did the same when we were kids and I gave her the world's worst excuses for whatever idiocy I had been up to that day.

She's not angry, like she used to be back then, though. If I had to hazard a guess, I'd say she's legitimately trying to make sense of what the two strangers are telling her.

"Who were you digging up?"

"Me!" Clothilde says helpfully from behind us. "I'm supposed to be the star here—everybody has just forgotten, apparently."

I turn to send a soft glare at her—we can't have her distracting Evian—and also to check that she is, indeed, joking.

"Don't worry, Robert," she says with her signature eye roll. "I'm happy to work on your case first. My time will come."

"I'm afraid we can't tell you that," Evian replies to Caroline. "But I can tell you that the two deaths seem to be linked."

"Do you know *how* he died?"

Licking her lips, Evian says, "It seems likely he was shot in the chest, probably straight through the heart."

Caroline stops breathing for a few seconds, her eyes going distant. Then she draws breath again—not a very deep one, but it's a breath. "So he probably didn't suffer for long?"

That all depends on what happened leading up to the bullet in my chest. And since I've forgotten everything that happened that day, even I don't know.

"Probably not," Evian replies, thankfully not taking my sister down the path of horrible possibilities when a police officer ends up dead.

"Does Maman know?"

Both officers nod and Doubira is the one to answer. "We talked to her yesterday. I take it from your reaction that she didn't tell you?"

"She's probably keeping it for our call tonight." Caroline sighs and takes her first sip of tea. It can't be very hot anymore. "We always talk once a week." Another sigh. "This is going to kill her."

I'm kind of afraid she's right. And not only in the metaphorical way.

Our mother was always a character to be reckoned with. She'd go up against ornery teachers and angry fathers during soccer practice alike. Nothing scared her.

Except losing her kids.

I don't think she intended me to hear, but I eavesdropped on her conversation with a close friend once, where she said she was convinced she could weather anything—except losing her kids.

No matter which one, she loved us all equally. And no matter if there would still be three left. She didn't think she'd be able to get past the mourning of the one she lost.

I was maybe fifteen at the time. I had rolled my eyes at my mother's melodrama and moved on with my life.

I remember how my mother deflated yesterday when she learned I was dead and suddenly I'm not very optimistic.

My sister takes another sip of her tea. This time she winces—she never did like her tea cold. "You say he was *buried*, though? In a casket? In a cemetery? Is that normal?"

Evian chuckles and pulls her teabag around in her cup by the thread. "Is there really such a thing as 'normal' when it comes to homicides? I've never worked a case where we found an *extra* body in the ground, but I have seen a body switch. They switched the bodies before the funeral and we only found out when we identified the body dumped in a river as a guy who was supposedly buried in a cemetery."

Caroline's lips twitch as Evian tells her anecdote and I'm grateful she's managed to lighten the mood a little. "Still. They got him a casket?"

"I'll admit I find that fascinating, too," Evian says. "However, it wasn't a pretty and fancy casket like the one in the real grave right next to him. It was more like a wooden box, probably made by the people who buried him."

"And you say there's a link between my brother and this other person?"

Evian bites her lips as she seems to consider her options. "He was working on the case of this person's death not too long before he disappeared."

"Oh." Caroline lets go of her cup and folds her hands in her lap. "That might explain it, then."

"Explain what?" Evian's eyes are laser sharp and Doubira doesn't seem to be missing much, either.

Caroline breathes a heartfelt sigh. "I don't think my brother was particularly good at his job," she says, her voice barely there. "He had a tendency to listen to the advice of the wrong people. I mostly helped him out when he got in trouble in high school, but once he started at the officers' school…"

Evian's voice is soft now. "Are you trying to tell us that your brother wasn't a very good cop?"

"Yes, that's exactly what I'm trying to tell you."

THIRTY-FOUR

WELL, OUCH.

It's true—I've known it for over thirty years. The fact that I was awful at my job while I was alive is the main reason I'm still here as a ghost—but still. Ouch.

"Are you basing your judgment on his behavior in high school or do you have proof he was the same fifteen years later?" Evian asks. "People *do* change and grow up."

Yeah, no, I didn't.

It took my own death for me to pull my head out of my ass.

Caroline shakes her head, her eyes sad. "Robert was my brother and I loved him dearly. He was so sweet and sensitive

168

as a boy. But I don't think he ever really found his place—in the family or in society."

She picks up her cup then puts it back down when she remembers the tea has gone cold. "There were four of us, and Robert was number three, one of three boys. Honestly, I think our parents did everything right, they gave us all the same amount of attention, but it was never enough for Robert. He was never the first to do something, he was never the strongest since he wasn't the biggest, and he wasn't the last or weakest either. I think he felt like he was just *there*. He wanted to be singled out. But our parents would never do that because it wouldn't have been fair to the rest of us.

"I don't think Robert ever realized that. That he *was* loved, that he *was* special—only not *more* special than the rest of us. So he sought validation elsewhere."

It *hurts* to sit here and listen to my own sister talking about me like this.

Even if it's true.

I never did feel like I was good enough. I wasn't sufficiently introspective to have put words to it like Caroline is doing now but I *didn't* feel seen by my parents or my siblings. There wasn't a single subject where, if someone needed help, they would think, "Oh, I know, I'll ask Robert."

We all want to feel appreciated and valued, right?

Caroline isn't done, of course. "I'm sure Robert could have made lots of friends in school, if he'd just been himself. He was smart, he was fast, he was strong, he was compassionate. But he didn't believe in himself, so he tried to emulate whoever he saw as role models.

"When you're a teenager, the boys that everyone else tend to look up to, because they're 'cool,' are the bullies. The loud guys.

And possibly the jocks. In Robert's school and year, the cool boys were mostly bullies."

Caroline runs a hand down her face. She's visibly tired and seems to have aged a year or two since we first came into her home. "Robert decided to do whatever it took to get into the cool gang, and started doing anything they asked him to do. I managed to stop him from going too far in bullying a boy two years younger than him once, but another time our parents were summoned by the director when he'd ruined some girl's homework by flushing it down the toilet."

I remember both of those occurrences and if I'd had any blood in my ghostly body, I would have flushed with shame. I'm glad Clothilde is sitting behind me so I don't have to meet her gaze right now.

Across from me, Doubira and Evian are listening intently, not interrupting, letting my sister tell her story at her own pace. I think Doubira is using his phone to record the conversation.

Looks like I was special, after all—I was the biggest loser.

"Our parents yelled at him," Caroline says. "Our older brother mocked him, our younger brother declared Robert was mean, and I tried to make him see that he should be making different friends. But nothing helped. He just got better at judging when he'd get caught and when he'd get away with it. He learned all the rules so he could know where to step to toe the line."

"Not exactly an ideal candidate for a police officer," Evian remarks.

"Not exactly, no," Caroline agrees. "But by the time he started training, I was busy with my own studies, making my own way in the world. When we were no longer in the same school, I didn't have as much insight into what he was doing and who he was hanging out with. I guess I assumed that since

I didn't hear of any other incidents from our parents, he had changed for the better."

"He got a law degree, right?" Doubira asks.

Caroline and I both nod. "Took him four years instead of three, but yes, he got a law degree. So he'd know all the rules of our society."

"And know how to toe the line," Evian finishes for her.

"This is *not* making you look good, dude," Clothilde comments from behind me.

"I told you I have things to atone for," I reply, my voice not quite steady.

She sighs and I know without looking that she's kicking her feet extra hard because she's annoyed. "You've atoned plenty by solving crimes out of a cemetery for thirty years. You're good, Robert. You're not supposed to pay for being an idiot for all eternity."

I love her for thinking that, and for saying it to me, but I don't agree.

The story Caroline is telling is only the beginning.

"I'm afraid I can't really tell you much more than that," Caroline says. "Little by little, we lost contact, especially when I got married and started a family."

"But you think he was still like this when he died?" Evian asks. "That he was prone to follow the lead of whoever he thought was 'the coolest'?"

Caroline looks out the window, to stare sightlessly at a small, blossoming cherry tree in the corner of her garden. "One can hope he pulled it together after a while. But the last time I saw him, he was very boisterous, telling everybody about his recent promotion and how he was sure he'd get another one really soon. He was still showing off, looking for approval. He *could* have simply been very good at his job. But it's just as likely that he'd hitched his wagon onto someone who promised him the moon."

Evian nods. Even though I know she can't actually see me, I'm having trouble looking at her eyes, afraid of eye contact. Having my character presented to her in such an abominable light makes me want to run and hide.

I want her to like me, to respect me.

Just like I wanted in high school, dammit. Will this never go away?

"I don't suppose he mentioned any names when he was bragging about his promotion?" Evian says.

"I'm afraid my memory isn't good enough to remember the details of a conversation I had thirty years ago, Madame," Caroline answers with a sad smile. "But I don't think so. I think he stayed vague, probably on purpose."

"Was he close with his brothers? Do you think they would know any names?"

I speak up to answer Evian. There's no point in having them waste time in visiting either of my brothers, even if I am curious about where they've ended up. "They'll know even less than Caroline. I never told them anything." For fear they would judge me and mock me.

"No," Caroline answers. "I don't think they'd be very helpful. I'm not sure if it's really a universal rule, but in our family, the whole 'men don't talk about their feelings' was a real thing. I'm not sure any of them would have ever really known each other if they hadn't had me as a mediator."

"Men," both Clothilde and Evian say in chorus.

Doubira chuckles in response but I hang my head.

Getting called out on being a loser sucks.

THIRTY-FIVE

To say I'm feeling under the weather during lunch and in the metro on our way back to the city center would be an understatement. I don't listen in on the officers' discussion and I don't respond to any of Clothilde's prodding.

I'm stuck in my head, going round in circles.

Circles I'm all too familiar with.

I spent my entire life feeling insignificant. Nobody really *saw* me. So I did my best to be seen, to get ahead. I will be the first to agree that my methods were far from perfect, but *I tried*.

And failed spectacularly.

Now, I already knew this. It's why I've hung around as a ghost for so long, because I'm convinced I need to atone for my past sins before I'll be allowed to move on to the afterlife. I knew it when I woke up as a ghost in my casket and came to terms with it before ever being released into the cemetery, where I met Clothilde.

But that was so long ago. Our lives in the cemetery might have been boring at times—there were only so many things to do in that place, after all—but I got on with my life. Quasi-afterlife. I forgot about the details of everything I had done and just moved on to work on the remedy.

Today I got all that history slapped in my face.

And it hurts.

Everybody I knew thought I was a loser. My bosses, who gave me orders to not do my job correctly, knowing perfectly well that was something I could deliver on. My *mom* thinking I never thought for myself and only followed others around blindly. My mom being *right* about that.

And now my sister. My beloved sister, who would always love me—who loved me *despite* of my constant feeling of inferiority.

I'm feeling *inferior*.

I growl in frustration and dig my hands into my hair, wishing I could feel the pull on my scalp. I'm on the metro with the others, standing halfway into a young student who's bopping his head to the rhythm of some rap I can barely hear from his earphones, not caring if he feels it or if I'm very obviously not part of the world of the living.

I'm dead, and insignificant, and incompetent.

"All right, that's enough!" Clothilde's yell makes me jump away from the young man with the earphones and straight into an elderly lady clutching a shopping bag to her chest.

Evian jerks straight and scans the people around her, looking for threats.

174

"Jeez, you scared the hell out of me," I tell Clothilde, a hand to my heart—not that it's been beating for the last thirty years.

"I've been trying to talk to you for ten minutes." Clothilde is also standing through someone but I can only see his bent legs sticking out of her knees, the rest of him is hidden behind her. "If talking doesn't get through, I'll yell."

"No need to get so angry. I needed some time to think."

"Think. *Think.*" She basically spits the word. Her eyes are blazing and her hair is moving as if she's standing in a storm. I've seen Clothilde angry before, but it's a rare occurrence. "What you're doing isn't *thinking*. It's *wallowing* in self-pity."

I take an unneeded breath to yell right back and tell her that's not true—except I realize it is.

So I shut my mouth.

Clothilde pokes a finger into my chest. "I thought you were better than this, Robert. I thought you'd *changed*. That's what you told me, right? That this stuff that everybody says about you, it was true back when you were alive? But when you died, you *changed* and now you're a better man, a better police officer. Right? Or have you been faking it for thirty years and now the real you is coming crashing back?"

I'm reeling. First everybody from my past paints the least flattering picture of me ever, and now Clothilde, the only person who knows the present me, is also weighing in?

I again take a deep breath. I'm not going to just take hit after hit like this and not fight back.

Then Clothilde's words register. She's not actually accusing me of being a bad person. She's accusing me of going *back* to being the loser that I used to be.

175

"Shit, you're right." I deflate and slump, to the point where Clothilde holds out a hand to make sure I don't fall to the floor. "I'm completely stuck in my head."

"Well, you need to get out of there," Clothilde says matter-of-factly. "It doesn't seem like it's a very good place to hang out. Come back here, to the present. And help us solve the case of your own murder, you idiot."

I chuckle at her affectionate insult.

I realize how lucky I am to have Clothilde with me for this adventure we've set out on. She's the only one who knows the real me, the person I've become as a ghost.

I don't know what I would have become if she hadn't been here to knock some sense into me. If she hadn't been here to *see* me.

Glancing over at Evian and Doubira, I see they've managed to grab seats next to each other and are having a whispered discussion with bent heads. They look like they're at ease with working together, like they trust each other.

I also wanted that trust. I wanted to be part of the group, part of a community. I wanted to be a trusted partner, someone they could count on.

When my character was smeared by everyone who knew me thirty years ago, that hope crumbled and died. Evian will never trust me, will never respect me. She might be able to hear me on some level because of her high sensitivity, but she is too smart to believe those feelings over all the other facts she's come across.

Me being me, I'd really like for her to like me. Give me her approval.

Yep, going round in circles again.

"I don't know how to get rid of this," I confide to Clothilde.

"You probably won't," she replies with a shrug. She's leaning close to the young man I was standing halfway through earlier, trying to listen in on his music. "Feelings suck, everybody knows that. You just gotta live with it."

I crack a smile. "That's your advice? Live with it?"

I'm treated to an eye roll and her gaze comes back to lock eyes with me. "Live with it. Deal with it. Don't let it hold you back. You can't live for other people's approval, Robert. Aim for your own. That's the only one that matters."

THIRTY-SIX

By the time they're back at the police station, the work day is almost over. Emeline asks Malik to find them a meeting room and get Nadine Tulle to join them. She can't put off telling the woman to stop looking into the dead girls any longer.

Malik delivers, and ten minutes later, they are seated around a scratched and worn table in a meeting room in the station's basement. Unfortunately there is no daylight, but Malik promises there is no way the room can be watched and the risk of someone dropping in on them is as good as non-existent.

Emeline can't quite figure out what got into her this afternoon but at least it seems to be calming down now. She was more excited than she should have been to meet with Robert Villemur's sister. Then, when Caroline painted her brother in such a bad light, Emeline was disappointed—a lot more than the situation warranted.

And on the metro ride back, she felt downright gloomy. Until she suddenly felt rather hopeful, for no apparent reason.

This case is messing with her head.

Not enough to stop her from working on it and giving it one hundred percent, though.

"We have some news for you," Emeline says to Nadine once they're all seated and the door is securely closed. "But if you don't mind, I'd like to first hear what you've found during your research."

"Sure." Nadine gives a sharp nod, making her blond braid jump against her chest. She opens the laptop she brought with her and types in a long password. "Have you had the chance to look at what I gave you yesterday?"

Emeline feels the beginnings of a blush but fights it back. "Sorry, no. I was too tired yesterday and today there hasn't really been time, especially if I want to use my personal computer."

"That's not a problem," Nadine says. "The data will still be there when you have the time to look at them. Do you have the USB drive with you?"

Emeline pats through her pockets. "Yes, I think so." She *did* put it in a pocket this morning, right? It's probably a good thing she made a bracelet of the finger bones, or she would have forgotten them somewhere by now.

"Ah, here it is." She pulls the small drive out of her pants pocket and hands it to Nadine.

"Great." The tiny woman makes quick work of fitting the drive into a slot. "I'll copy over the stuff I found today, so now you have everything." As she hands the drive back, she looks between Emeline and Malik with a gleam in her eye. "Would you like a quick run-down of my findings?"

"That's why we're here, Tulle," Emeline says and adds in a smile to take the sting out of her words. It's not even five in the afternoon but she's already getting too tired to be overly diplomatic.

It's a good thing Spangero caught her in the morning, all things considered.

Nadine folds her laptop closed, apparently not needing it for support. "First, about the girls who were ruled as suicides. I've added to both the raw data and the findings.

"I believe I've found all the deaths that *could* be victims of the same serial killer, going all the way back to 1988. I even tried searching a little earlier and found a couple of hits the year before, but nothing before 1987. In my opinion, that's the time when the whole thing started."

Emeline nods but doesn't interrupt. The woman is good. She was told not to go beyond Clothilde Humbert's time of death, but had extended her search a little further anyway and might have found a very important clue. If they could find the *first* victim, that was sure to help understand the origin of the murders and the murderer alike.

"I've retrieved all the data I could on all the cases," Nadine continues. "And cross-referenced pretty much everything. By taking into account the likeliness that the girl had, in fact, committed suicide, the opinions of the family and friends, the names of the officers working the case and seeing if they were involved in any other suspect cases, the location the girl was found in, and the speed at which the case was opened and closed, I've extracted a list of thirty-four victims that I consider likely to have been the victims of our serial killer. Fifteen of the victims you had exhumed earlier are on the list. The rest have been excluded because they did not meet all the criteria."

She folds her hands on top of her laptop. Emeline suspects she does it to avoid that nervous habit of pulling on her hair. "I've also added information to the file on Robert Villemur," Nadine says. "The guy seems to have been a follower, dating all the way back to high school."

Emeline's eyebrows once again shoot up in surprise. No wonder the woman's nervous. They're not supposed to have access to this kind of information, especially since Villemur was a minor at the time and didn't have a criminal record. Some minor vandalism isn't enough to open his files.

She decides not to say anything. The information is too valuable. And ignorance is bliss.

"So I've compiled a list of all the people whose orders he might have followed, especially over the last three to five years before he disappeared," Nadine says. "You'll have all his direct bosses, but also the ones he was rumored to have spent time with."

She clenches her fingers and licks her lips. "I collected some information on who he spent the most time with in that last year before his disappearance. A couple of them are still active, so it might be worth it to talk to them."

Emeline narrows her eyes at the young woman. "You can't possibly have found that last information in our system. Did you call someone?" If she did, Emeline needed to know, so she'd be aware of not having the element of surprise.

Another lick of the lips. "I talked to the guy who was his partner at the time. I didn't tell him Villemur's body had been found, or anything about the investigation, really. I'm pretty sure he thinks we're looking into a case that his partner might have been involved with at the time."

"Which is exactly what we're doing," Emeline says.

"Right. Yes." She gives up on the folded hands and reaches up to throw her braid over her shoulder. "I'm sorry if I gave away too much. I hope I haven't ruined anything for you. But I got the feeling he had things to say about Villemur so I gave him a crumb. And you'll definitely want to talk to him—he seems convinced his partner was involved in something illegal before he died."

Emeline pushes back the disappointment at Tulle having made her first mistake. It happens to everyone, at one point or another in their career, when the enthusiasm to solve the case takes the upper hand. She probably wanted to please Emeline and Malik—and she genuinely seems to know she went a step too far. Berating her won't do any good.

"I'll find the name of the person in your report?" Emeline asks.

Nadine nods.

"Okay. Now, to our news." Emeline takes a deep breath and lets it out slowly. She isn't sure how much to share with Nadine. She shares everything from this case with Malik because he's her partner. If she doesn't trust him, she won't be able to do her job.

But Nadine is more of an outsider. She's very good at doing research but she's not part of the Judicial Police force. Doubira clearly trusts her but she's very young, even younger than him.

Emeline decides to share but to keep some distance. Tulle will have to prove herself over time. "The case of the wrongly ruled suicides will have to be put on hold for a little while," she says. "I'm sure we'll be getting back to it in no time, but right now the focus is on the upcoming trial of Monsieur de Villenouvelle, and the six girls we know he raped and probably killed. We'll let that case run its course and once it's done, we'll get back to the other similar cases."

Tulle looks upset, like she's about to ask why. To avoid saying outright that she has decided not to share the information, Emeline pretends not to notice, and plows ahead.

"We *will*, however, look into the death of Robert Villemur. I intend to find out how he died and what, if any, his relationship was with Clothilde Humbert. There's a reason they were buried together, I'm absolutely sure of it. I'm sure we'll be needing your help again in the future—if you're still willing to help?"

Tulle isn't happy. But to her credit, she lets the subject go. So she knows to read people well enough to realize Emeline won't be answering any questions. Good. That's not always the case with the people who choose to spend their lives searching for information on computers instead of out amongst people.

"Of course I'll help," she replies, her voice a little unsteady. "I'd never leave a project hanging. If you need *anything*, let me know."

Tulle's cheeks are red and her breathing has sped up. She's working up to asking Emeline about the murdered girls anyway.

"Good," Emeline says forcefully. "Then I guess we're done here." She holds up the USB drive before shoving it back into the pocket it came from. "Thank you very much for your valuable help. It will not be forgotten."

And then she walks out of the room so quickly that Doubira knocks his chair to the ground in his hurry to follow.

THIRTY-SEVEN

ARE WE GOING to see Stéphane? That was his name, right?

I can't believe I don't even remember the name of the guy I partnered with for at least three or four months.

I'm assuming that's who Tulle was talking about, because my partner before Stéphane was a woman and Tulle definitely said "he."

"So your partner was yet another person who didn't like you, huh?" Clothilde says as we follow Evian and Doubira through the dark corridors of the police station basement.

"Guess that shouldn't be a surprise by now," I reply glumly. It actually takes me a while to really take in the information Tulle gave us. I've gotten so used to everybody from my past dumping on my character, this just felt like one more to add to the pile.

"He didn't only say I was a loser and a follower." I stop walking as the realization hits but Evian ruins the effect by walking up the staircase and letting the door slam shut behind her. I get sucked past the door after her.

Clothilde is waiting for me on the other side of the door, arms crossed and a bored expression on her youthful face. "So?"

"He thinks I was involved in something *criminal.*" I really want to stay immobile for this conversation, take a stand, physically show my shock and indignation—but Evian is opening the door on the next floor so I hurry after her to avoid getting pulled through again. It's not a feeling I want to get used to.

Once we're in the open-plan office and Evian and Doubira go to their desks, presumably to do some paperwork, I can finally focus. "Stéphane told Tulle that I might have gotten killed because I was involved in something illegal," I say to Clothilde.

"Who's Stéphane?"

"My partner."

"Oh, okay. Continue." She jumps up on the closest desk and shoves her hands under her thighs.

I'm a little miffed that she doesn't show more interest before remembering that this is *Clothilde*, the ultimate teenager. Of course she won't show interest.

"Well, we've spent the last couple of days listening to my family and official records saying I couldn't think for myself, that I was a follower, and an all-round loser. It could sound like I walked into a situation I couldn't get out of because I was too stupid to see and judge the danger. Painting me as a *bad guy* is new."

Clothilde shrugs. "Wouldn't it be possible to be involved in something illegal without realizing it? If you follow the bad guy, does that make you a bad guy?"

It makes you stupid. But I guess we've already established that, so I do my best to brush the thought away.

"I guess that's a possibility. In a certain sense, it's *true*, since I blindly followed orders—*suggestions*—to open and close several cases in about five seconds flat. That makes me incompetent, and stupid, but I'm not sure I'd qualify it as illegal. The way Tulle said it, it sounded like I was actively working against the law."

Clothilde cocks her head as she stares at me, her big eyes never blinking. I have all her attention now, and the sullen teenager is nowhere to be seen.

"*Did* you ever break the law?" she asks.

I force down the disappointment and anger that tries to rise at my one and only friend making accusations.

She's *not* accusing me. She's trying to understand. My emotions are simply a little slow on the uptake.

I force myself to meet her gaze. "I probably cut a few corners. Everybody does. I probably learned the rules so I could know how far to toe the line without actually crossing over. But I can't remember ever doing anything that I should have been arrested for. I was lazy, and incompetent, and insecure—but a *criminal*?"

"Every criminal has a moment when they step too far over the line, right?" Clothilde says. "The point of no return? Is it possible this happened for you during your last days and you got killed for it?"

Was I *that* incompetent, even as a criminal?

"You really don't remember the day you died?" Clothilde asks.

I shake my head. "Honestly, I can't really pinpoint what my last memory even is. I know I remember going to your crime scene. I know I don't remember Gisèle Grand's crime scene at all. Those two were less than a couple of weeks apart, right?"

"I think so, yes."

"Stéphane and I were investigating some boring-ass stuff on the theft of really expensive and old jewelry from an abbey outside of town, but I mostly just followed along and let him do the work. I don't see a link between that and the murders at all."

I run my hand through my hair in a nervous gesture that is apparently back to stay as I do my best to remember what I was doing during my last weeks of life thirty years ago.

"Some of those days blend together in my mind," I say with a sigh. "And not because something happened to my memory but because I found that case so horribly boring." It wasn't going to get me anywhere career-wise—as opposed to what Montbleu promised me if I followed his instructions.

As I work through all the old memories, one realization is clear. "I don't remember *anything* about intending to go against the law. If I did make that decision, it came suddenly and had immediate consequences. And it really does feel out of character." I wouldn't have had the guts to take such risks. The shame at getting caught would have been too great.

"Then why did this partner of yours think you did something illegal?"

I take a deep breath and square my shoulders in an attempt to show a confidence in my own character that I don't really feel. "That's what we need to find out."

I glance over at Evian, who is closing up her computer and telling Doubira good night with a squeeze of his shoulder as she walks past.

I hope she is as good as she seems. I hope she won't give up on finding out what happened to me thirty years ago. I know she also wants to go into the details of the murder of Clothilde and who knows how many other young girls, and so do I, but

I'm kind of relieved that she's being forced to look into my case first.

I'm used to feeling inferior, insecure. Feeling judged by everyone I meet. Or rather, I *was* used to it. Thirty years in a cemetery with Clothilde and lots of cases to solve made me forget about the past. At least enough to feel like I made a difference in the world, like I mattered.

Going back to being the loser is killing me—not literally, of course, but what the hell happens to a depressive ghost? That sounds like an awful way to spend eternity.

As we follow Evian out of the police station and through the busy streets of Toulouse, I make a silent promise to myself.

I'll allow myself to be selfish enough to focus first on my own past and murder. If I don't, I won't be able to give my complete focus to anything. Once I know what happened—no matter which side of the law I land on—I'm dedicating everything I have to helping Evian and Doubira look into the girls' murders.

As long as Evian lets me come along for the ride.

THIRTY-EIGHT

THE EVENING IS oddly calm and uneventful. Evian walks home, clearly lost in her own thoughts as she strolls down sidewalks at a very leisurely pace, not really looking at anything or anyone.

Clothilde takes the opportunity to test our bond with her. She walks ahead or stays behind but never goes farther than fifty meters from Evian. She says it becomes very uncomfortable and that if she *had to*, she probably could go farther, but not much. The pull toward Evian—or rather toward our finger bones in that bracelet—is too strong.

Back in her apartment, Evian shucks off her shoes by the door and hangs her jacket over a chair. She removes the bracelet and places it on the kitchen counter before going to her room to change into a pair of worn jeans and a black t-shirt.

Then she sits on her worn couch, looking at the USB drive that Tulle gave her.

Not looking at the data on her computer. Looking at the drive as she turns it over and over in her hand.

I might not be a computer whiz but I'm pretty sure she won't be reading the report like that.

When the clock on the microwave approaches eight, Evian places the little drive on the kitchen counter next to the bracelet and starts cooking dinner. It's a simple pasta dish, with white sauce and canned mushrooms, but it looks absolutely delicious.

Clearly, not being able to eat is going to be our favorite kind of torture. Clothilde and I both settle in next to Evian and follow each mouthful with envious eyes. We're both reminded—again—of how much we love food.

Once the dishes are gone, Evian returns to the couch, this time with her laptop and the USB drive. Finally, we're going to learn what Tulle discovered.

Physical realm be damned, Clothilde and I both settle down three-quarters into the couch, so that we may have a good view of Evian's screen. Only our heads and shoulders protrude from the couch.

There are two folders: one named *Ruled Suicides*, the other *R. Villemur*.

Evian hovers the mouse over the suicide folder but she doesn't click on it. She opens the folder with my name on it, bypasses completely the file named "data" and clicks to open the one called "report."

It holds a lot of names, many of which we've already heard. De Villenouvelle, Montbleu, Stéphane, Durand, Gisèle Grand,

Clothilde Humbert. No other girls' names with the tag "ruled suicide," so it seems like Tulle couldn't find a link to any of the other victims.

I think that's a good thing.

Clothilde sucks in a breath. Evian's hand jerks slightly on the mouse she has perched on her thigh and looks around the empty room before shaking her head and huffing.

"What is it?" I ask Clothilde.

She points to the very last line of the report. "Laurent Lambert."

I lean in to read the single line of text. *In last report before disappearance: planned to question Laurent Lambert in relation to Gisèle Grand's death.*

I lean back in surprise and almost disappear into the couch. I catch myself and float up to pretend to sit on the lousy piece of furniture next to Evian. "It looks like I was actually going to investigate the murder of Mademoiselle Grand." I lean forward to meet Clothilde's eyes. "That's what it looks like, right?"

There's anger in her eyes but it seems like her desire to mock me is stronger. She rolls her eyes at me, Clothilde style. "You're the detective, Robert. You tell me."

The hope rising within me at the prospect of having done *something* right, even if it resulted in my death, is strong. If I'd had a beating heart, it would have been pounding in my chest. "That's what it looks like," I whisper.

Evian also seems to have latched onto the name. Either because it rings a bell or because her subconscious heard us. She opens the *Ruled Suicides* folder and types Laurent Lambert's name into a search bar at the top of the screen.

She opens the first file in the list of results and three seconds later we're looking at Clothilde's name on the screen. *Room rented by lawyer Laurent Lambert but nothing could be proved and he had an alibi for the time of death.*

"Gotcha," Evian says, a satisfied tilt to her lips. "Monsieur Lambert is the link between the two deaths."

She doesn't spend much more time on the data that Tulle gave her. I get the feeling she doesn't want to look too closely at the information on the ruled suicides. Either because she doesn't want to be tempted to spend too much time on it or because the big boss told her not to. I'm leaning toward the first option.

Which means we'll be getting back to the girls once we figure out what happened to me—an agenda I'm more than on board with.

Evian spends some time searching for information on Laurent Lambert. The first point is that he's still alive.

Clothilde growls at that discovery, even though we already knew he'd met both Lise and Manon before they died.

We also learn that he owns a legal practice with offices in the most expensive part of the city center, not too far from the City Hall. He doesn't seem to take on any direct cases himself any longer. He probably leaves the actual work to employees while he's out plotting the murder of innocent young women.

Or something.

Evian types the legal office's number into her phone, as well as the address. Then she sends off a message requesting a meeting during lunch hour tomorrow.

She spends some more time searching for information, both on Stéphane and on Lambert but she doesn't come up with much. After rubbing her eyes for the fourth time in five minutes, she switches off the computer and places it on the coffee table.

She's about to put the little USB drive back in her pocket when she stops, and apparently changes her mind.

She goes to the center of the room and does a slow turn, studying her living room from top to bottom. She finds what she's looking for in the bookcase in the corner.

Evian hasn't brought any books, of course, but it looks like previous tenants left whatever they didn't want to take with them, so it's filled with various trinkets, weird decorations, travel books, thrillers, and baby books that seem to have been eaten and digested by whatever baby used to live here.

On the second shelf from the top, one of those Japanese cats with a moving arm stands, face turned toward the back of the bookcase. It has lost its moving arm so it's just a weird and colorful cat with a hole on the side.

Evian takes the cat down, studies it for a moment, then slips the USB drive into the hole. It clanks twice as it goes in. With a satisfied nod, Evian puts the cat back in the bookshelf, turned so the hole in the side isn't too obvious.

Then she spends the rest of the evening on the couch, with a cup of herbal tea in one hand and a novel in the other.

Clothilde crouches next to the couch, trying to read over Evian's shoulder but I'm not sure she's very successful. Every time Evian turns a page, Clothilde makes a whining noise.

"Is she a faster reader than you, Clothilde?" I ask with a smile.

"I'm out of practice," she practically growls. "I've read nothing but tombstones for thirty years." She stops talking as she leans forward trying to read the bottom of the current page before it disappears.

"I miss reading stories," she whispers. "And this is a good one."

Giving her a genuine smile this time, I say, "I won't distract you. Practice your reading skills. Enjoy the story."

She doesn't reply but her lips are set in a determined line and I have no doubt she'll be able to keep up with Evian in no time.

I might be mistaken but I think that the next time she finishes a page, Evian takes a little break to take a sip of her tea before turning the page.

THIRTY-NINE

THE NEXT MORNING Evian takes the car again. She grumbles to herself behind the wheel all the way to the police station, where she picks up Doubira, and then she grumbles a bit louder as she drives them out of the city toward the north.

When we worked together, Stéphane lived in a two-bedroom apartment not too far from the police station. Life seems to have treated him well; he now lives in a relatively large house with a huge expanse of neatly cut lawn, a swing set, and several fruit trees on the outskirts of one of the many villages surrounding Toulouse.

It's calm. It's beautiful. It's remote.

It's not at all how I would have pictured Stéphane's home.

195

Neither Doubira nor Evian have called ahead to tell my old partner they are coming but he doesn't seem particularly surprised when they're at his door. He must have seen it coming after whatever Tulle told him on the phone yesterday.

While Evian introduces herself and her partner, I take the opportunity to study Stéphane.

Thirty years is a really long time. Especially when you yourself have been frozen in time and stuck in a tiny cemetery. I think I'd somehow assumed that nobody on the outside, the people who were still alive, changed any more than I did.

My mother's an old lady, my sister is well beyond middle-aged. And my partner, who was just past forty when I died in 1988, is now...I make a quick mental calculation...seventy-six. Jeez, he looks it, too.

He still has hair on his head but it's completely white and so thin I can see the numerous marks the sun has left on his scalp. His nose seems bigger and is covered in busted veins and he's wearing glasses that he didn't need when I worked with him. His skin is darkly tanned, with wrinkles so deep around the eyes, they can qualify as folds.

But it's still Stéphane, and his voice is the same—a tiny little bit higher than you'd expect from his physique.

"I talked to your colleague yesterday," he says. "There's some news about Robert?"

"Yes, there is," Evian says. "Would you mind inviting us in so we can talk?"

"Certainly." Stéphane lets them in but doesn't offer anything to drink, hot or cold. I'm honestly a little surprised because he never appeared to be awkward in social interactions when we worked together.

Stéphane leads Evian and Doubira into his living room. He stands in the middle of the room, not going near any of the chairs at the dining table by the large bay windows or the couches by the gorgeous open fireplace, so everybody else remains standing as well.

Except Clothilde, who perches on the dining table.

"What exactly did our colleague tell you yesterday?" Evian asks, her voice gently curious, like she's asking only to save him the trouble of getting the same information twice.

Stéphane shrugs and crosses his arms, making his checkered shirt pull across the beginnings of a beer gut. "Not much. Only that you were looking into a case that Robert was working on before he died."

Evian's eyebrows shoot up and Doubira is about to say something but he catches the look on his partner's face in time so he shuts his mouth immediately.

"Nadine Tulle didn't tell him they found your body, did she?" Clothilde asks me in a whisper.

I shake my head, never letting my eyes leave Stéphane's face.

"I assume it's about that dead girl?" Stéphane doesn't seem to notice the reactions of the people around him, even the alive and visible ones.

"That dead girl," Evian says. Her voice is flat but it's clearly a question for Stéphane to elaborate.

Stéphane doesn't resist for long in the silence that follows. That's a trick he clearly still hasn't learned. "I don't remember her name. It was too long ago. But there was a young woman who committed suicide and we were the first officers on the scene. It was just before Robert disappeared, that's the only reason I remember it."

"You get *that* many young women who commit suicide?" Doubira asks and I can't tell from his voice if he really is asking the question and wondering if he'll end up seeing so many dead people he becomes jaded, or if he's playing a part to get more information out of Stéphane.

"There have been more than one," Stéphane answers gruffly. Defensively. "But that's not how I meant it. I meant that I remember it being the last crime scene I worked with Robert."

"Before he died," Evian says.

"Yes." Another silence and this time Stéphane holds out longer. I think he might be catching on that this isn't going too well, and in the end that's what makes him keep talking. To defend himself.

"It leaves a mark when you lose a partner. So you think back on the last things you did together, both to remember them by and to search for answers. One day we were working together and the next he was gone. That kind of thing leaves a mark. I've forgotten many things in my old age but I remember every little detail of the last time I saw Robert."

Evian nods in agreement. "I understand. When exactly *was* the last time you saw Monsieur Villemur?"

Stéphane opens his mouth to reply, then hesitates. "I wouldn't want to take up too much of your precious time with my memories of an old friend. I thought you were here to look into Gisèle Grand's death?" His arms remain folded across his chest and he's becoming more tense by the second.

"Ah, I see you remembered her name," Evian says genially, as if she's simply happy that his memories are coming back to him. "We are looking into an old case. I didn't say it was Mademoiselle Grand's death."

"Whatever else could it be?" Stéphane blurts out.

"Did you not work on any other cases at the time of your partner's disappearance?" Doubira asks.

"Of course we did. There was always some sort of big thing we were working on in the background while we waited for the next emergency. But you can't expect me to remember what case we were working at that specific time thirty years ago."

Silence again.

Clothilde doesn't bother to whisper this time. "Is his memory going because he's so old or is he just really bad at lying?"

"Could be both," I reply. But I'm leaning toward the second option.

Which is all kinds of interesting.

This time Stéphane holds out against the silence and Evian is the one to break it.

"We have indeed come across the case of Mademoiselle Grand," she says. "But we were originally looking into the death of Clothilde Humbert."

"Me!" Clothilde exclaims, a huge smile on her face.

"Stop it," I tell her. "You're going to distract Evian." But I can't stop a smile from spreading across my face.

"Oh. Her." I can't be entirely sure because of his tan, but I think Stéphane's face has lost some color.

"Excellent, you remember her." Evian looks to Doubira, pretending confusion. "I didn't think Villemur had his partner with him for that case."

"Not according to the files I saw," Doubira replies smoothly.

Evian turns to Stéphane. "Are the files mistaken?"

Stéphane uncrosses his arms and seems to stop himself from drying his palms on his pants and settles for placing his hands on his hips instead, making him look even more awkward.

"I wasn't at the crime scene with him," he says. "But Robert told me about it after."

"It must have been quite the case, for you to remember it so well thirty years later, and not having worked it yourself."

"Well. No. It was just another suicide."

"A memorable one." Evian's tone is that of a statement but it's also clearly a question.

"Yes." Stéphane's breathing has shortened and his eyes keep darting between Evian and Doubira, as if judging his chances if he runs for the hills. "It was clearly memorable to Robert, which is why he mentioned it to me, and that's why I remember it."

"All right." Evian flashes a perfunctory smile to signal that line of questioning is over and Stéphane deflates in relief.

How he survived an entire career as a cop is something of a mystery right now.

He seems to realize his mistake when Evian asks her next question.

"You seem to work under the assumption that Robert Villemur is dead?"

Stéphane was in the process of returning his arms across his chest and now he freezes, making him look like a terrible ballerina halfway into a pose. "I, uh… Honestly, I just always assumed he was dead. A man like Robert doesn't simply take off like that without telling anyone. If he didn't come back, it's because he couldn't."

"He could have been kidnapped." Doubira is mimicking Evian, standing at parade rest and rocking slowly back and forth.

"I said I made the assumption." Stéphane's voice is close to a whisper. "Is he not dead?"

"Oh, he's dead," Evian says genially. "In fact, we found his body when we exhumed Mademoiselle Humbert."

"*That's* where—" Stéphane catches himself and tries again. "That's terrible! Do you know how he died?"

"Oh, yes. The bullet that killed him was still lodged in his spine. I expect feedback on the ballistics within a day or two. Isn't that so, Doubira?"

Doubira lifts up on his toes and lets himself fall back down. "Yes. Possibly by the end of the day."

I'm seriously worried Stéphane will die of a heart attack right before our eyes. I'm not entirely sure he's still breathing and I can see his erratic pulse in his neck from across the room.

"This is absolutely fascinating," I say to nobody in particular.

Clothilde eyes me with an odd look in her eye. "You're taking this very well. Seeing how you reacted when your family described you, I'd expect a little more of a reaction here."

Not sure what it says about me that I'm more comfortable with my partner clearly having been involved in my murder in one way or another than with my family describing me as a follower. But it's true.

Except for the fact that I would, obviously, rather not have been murdered thirty years ago, I really couldn't care less that Stéphane had something to do with it.

Unless he was the one to pull the trigger?

Possibly not even then. Stéphane was like me—he followed. If he had anything to do with my death, it's because he followed orders.

"The officer who called you yesterday told me you seemed to be of the opinion that your partner was involved in something illegal before he disappeared," Evian says.

The relief in Stéphane's expression is pathetic. "Yes! That's why I assumed he was dead. He got involved with the wrong people and when they weren't happy with him, they turned on him."

That's oddly detailed.

Evian seems to think so, too. "Do you know *who* these people were? What kind of illegal activity he was involved in?"

Stéphane shakes his head so hard his jowls shake. "I wouldn't know. If I did, I would have turned him in. I just got the feeling he was doing some shady stuff on the side."

Another silence settles. Evian looks around Stéphane's living room, very obviously studying the nice furniture and the large expanse of lawn visible outside the large bay windows.

"Anyway," she says as if suddenly remembering she has a job to do. "We should probably get going. We have other people to talk to today." She takes two steps toward the door, stops and turns back to Stéphane.

"By the way, you wouldn't happen to know a lawyer named Laurent Lambert?"

Stéphane shakes his head. Vigorously.

Yeah, he knows him.

FORTY

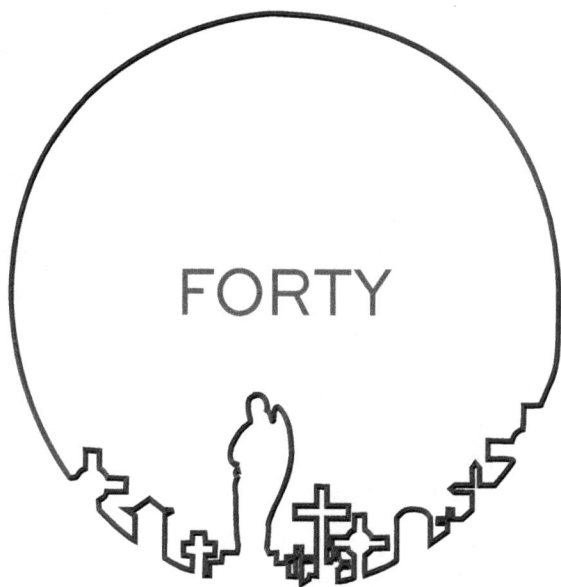

"SHOULDN'T WE BRING him in for questioning?" Malik asks as they get back in the car.

"We will," Emeline replies. She takes her time buckling up and turning the ignition while keeping an eye on Stéphane Petit's home. "I want to see what he does when he panics first."

There's isn't even a question of whether or not the man *will* panic. He will. He was already panicking before Emeline and Malik were out the door.

Clearly the man knew more than he should about Robert Villemur's demise—but did he just know something or had he been involved in the murder himself? Also, how could nobody else have figured anything out before now?

Being a good liar isn't exactly a criteria to become a police officer—but following the training on interrogation techniques definitely is, even back in the eighties. Either the man is losing his touch—big time—with age, or he's never been the sharpest knife in the drawer.

Which brings Emeline back to the question of how this went undetected for so long. Did nobody question Villemur's partner?

Emeline can feel them closing in on answers concerning Robert Villemur's death—but she has a feeling they'll end up with an even longer list of new questions.

No matter. She'll figure it out, one question at a time.

Malik checks his watch. "Didn't you say you have a meeting in the city at noon?"

The clock on the dashboard reads a quarter past eleven. With the traffic they're bound to run into, they have to take off.

Emeline pulls out of Stéphane Petit's driveway and directs the car toward Toulouse. "We'll have to come back to check on Petit. Or simply bring him in for questioning. I don't think he'll be too hard to break."

Malik chuckles. "No kidding."

Emeline pulls to a stop at a light. As the light turns green, something brings her to look in the rearview mirror. About a hundred meters back, a black BMW comes out of a side street. The same street they just came from.

"Did you happen to see the type of car Petit drove?" she asks as she accelerates. She watches the road but checks for the BMW in the mirror every five seconds. It rolls through the intersection right before the light turns red.

"A black BMW," Malik answers. After a glance at Emeline, he turns in his seat to look behind them. His tone turns incredu- lous. "Is he following us?"

"There aren't *that* many roads out of this village. He could just be going out."

"Yeah, right. Someone freaks me out about a murder that happened thirty years ago and I'll go, 'Hey, I think I'll go shopping.' Do you think he thinks he's being smooth? I mean, we couldn't possibly miss seeing him."

Emeline stops checking the mirror every few seconds now that Malik is keeping an eye on the BMW. "Who knows what's going through his head right now. Sometimes, when people are too stupid, I find it hard to anticipate their movements."

Malik chuckles again. He stays turned backward as Emeline makes a left turn to take one of the larger roads in the direction of Toulouse. The traffic isn't exactly dense but it has enough cars that someone like Stéphane Petit should have trouble keeping track of a car as common as the one Emeline is driving.

He manages to keep track.

Emeline makes several turns, aiming for the highway leading back to Toulouse, and Petit makes the exact same turns.

"Could he have been faking the whole idiot thing?" Malik asks. "He's following even when he couldn't possibly have seen us turn."

Emeline is starting to have some doubts, too. She arrives at the toll station and on a whim, instead of driving through, she pulls into the small parking lot to the side. A huge trailer is already parked there and she makes sure to pick a parking spot behind it so she won't be visible to any cars coming into the toll station.

Less than a minute later, the black BMW drives straight through the gate for subscription passes and accelerates onto the highway toward Toulouse. He never sees Emeline and Malik in their little rental, and doesn't seem bothered to have lost them.

"He's not following us," Emeline says and hurries to pull out of the parking. "He's simply going the same direction."

"He couldn't even wait until we were out of sight to take off?"

Yes, Stéphane Petit is apparently *that* stupid. Or that panicked.

Emeline speeds through the toll booth, barely letting the barrier open before she floors it and lets the little car do its best at catching up to the larger BMW.

"I take it we're not going to see Laurent Lambert?" Malik's voice is calm but his right hand is clutching the car door so hard his knuckles are white.

"We're not late yet," Emeline says. "If we can manage not to lose him, we'll see where he's going. Then we'll see if we can make the meeting with Lambert or if we should reschedule." She went a little over the speed limit for the first five hundred meters or so but she soon caught sight of the black car and now she's cruising just below the speed limit two to three cars behind Petit.

She's not particularly worried he'll spot them.

Petit takes the exit toward Toulouse and proceeds in the direction of the city center. In order to make sure not to lose sight of him, Emeline places herself so that only one car separates her from Petit's. She suspects she could have been right behind him and he wouldn't have noticed.

"He never looks in his rearview mirror," Malik comments. "This guy was a *cop*?"

Petit's car stops so suddenly the car behind him almost runs right into him. As it becomes clear Petit intends to parallel park in an open spot, the car behind him pulls around, freely hitting the horn.

"Looks like we've arrived," Emeline says. She also drives past the BMW. Even Petit will have to look behind him if he's going to parallel park.

"There's another spot down there." Malik points and Emeline sees the spot. It's barely longer than the car but Emeline didn't grow up in Paris for nothing. She parks the car in two maneuvers, leaving them waiting while Petit fits his much larger car into his spot.

"Isn't that the City Hall down the road?" Emeline asks. She's not very familiar with the city yet but recognizes the majestic brick building with the French flag above the main entrance.

"Yes," Malik answers. "In fact, Laurent Lambert's office is down that street back there." His voice trails off and his eyes widen as his gaze meets Emeline's. "You asked if he knew Lambert. You think... Come on." He turns in his seat to better see Petit as he exits his car.

And takes off down the side street Malik just pointed out.

"Really?" His incredulity is bordering on comic and if it wasn't suddenly *very* important not to lose sight of Petit, Emeline would have made fun of him.

"Looks like it," she says and jumps out of the car. "Let's go."

FORTY-ONE

WE ALL TAKE off after Stéphane. Evian and Doubira draw some stares because of their hurry and focus, but Stéphane, being up ahead and never so much as glancing behind him, doesn't notice.

He runs straight into a large building of gray stately stones and huge ancient wooden doors. The plaque by the door reads *Laurent Lambert.*

"So we'll be on time for the meeting after all. Awesome!" Clothilde's tone is her usual lighthearted one but the look on her face is anything but. Her hair is moving as if it's affected by the slight breeze flowing through the inner courtyard of Lambert's building and her eyes look ancient and angry.

Evian and Doubira jog after Stéphane, across the courtyard and up two flights of stairs. Clothilde and I are close behind.

We find the door to Lambert's office open and the even-higher-than-usual voice of Stéphane seeping out. Evian stops right by the door where she won't be seen by anyone on the inside and makes a sign for Doubira to do the same.

Being invisible to whoever is inside, I move into the office. Since the door is open, I don't need to stay in the same room as Evian. I just can't move too far away from her.

Stéphane is at the reception desk, red-faced and yelling at the poor receptionist, a young man in his early twenties with hipster glasses and a crisply ironed salmon-colored shirt.

"I need to see Maître Lambert *right now*. It's an emergency! Is he here? I *know* he's here."

"Maître Lambert isn't available right now," the receptionist says with admirable poise. "He is finishing up a phone call and then he has another appointment coming in at noon."

"I don't *care* if he has another meeting. This is *urgent*. Did you not hear me? I have to see him *now*!"

Stéphane's volume keeps increasing with every word and on the last sentence he's yelling at the poor receptionist. I can see drops of spit flying and Stéphane's face is so red I'm worried he might have a stroke.

Not that I'd care overly much if he dies but I want to get to the bottom of this case first. I want to know what his involvement in my own death was.

Then he can croak for all I care.

I would have expected Clothilde to stand close to Stéphane and make fun of him in one way or another. But all trace of humor has clearly left for the day and her face is perfectly serious as she presses her ear to the door that has Lambert's name on it.

209

"Putting my ear to the wood doesn't make any difference," she says, annoyed. "There isn't even a keyhole for me to look through."

The door flies open and Clothilde jumps back. Some reflexes never go away, even after thirty years as a ghost.

The man who appears in the doorway looks to be in his sixties with a short impeccable haircut, a set of wire-rimmed glasses, and what I'm willing to bet is a very expensive gray suit that *almost* hides his paunch. He doesn't say anything but sends a death glare at Stéphane and makes a cut-it motion across his neck.

"I knew he was here!" Stéphane says to the receptionist. His voice is back to a more normal level but Lambert's silent instructions clearly weren't enough to shut him up completely. By the look on the receptionist's face, this is shocking behavior.

"I need to talk to you," Stéphane says, taking two steps toward Lambert. "The *police* came by my house this—"

"Shut it," Lambert whispers sharply. Stéphane hears it, the receptionist hears it, but Evian and Doubira on the landing outside probably don't. "They're in the building. You must leave *now*."

Clothilde appears at my side next to Stéphane. "He shouldn't get to leave, should he?"

"No. Having them both here is a very good thing."

"Emeline!" Clothilde yells, making me jump. "Time to make an entrance!"

Bless that woman and her sensitivity. Before Lambert has Stéphane halfway to a door labeled as a meeting room, Evian steps through the door, Doubira scrambling in behind her.

"Monsieur Petit," she says in that genial tone that I'm coming to recognize as something between anger and sarcasm. "Imagine running into you here. You *did* say you'd never met Maître

Lambert, no? When we talked less than thirty minutes ago? Did I get that wrong?"

Stéphane stands frozen, his mouth hanging open and his eyes wide with panic.

"You must be Maître Lambert." Evian walks up to the man and extends a hand. "We have an appointment at noon. Emeline Evian. I'm afraid I'm five minutes early. The traffic was lighter than expected." She says this with a smile that I think is genuine.

Lambert keeps his cool much better than Stéphane but it still takes him a second or two too many to shake Evian's hand. "Laurent Lambert. *Enchanté.*"

There's something vaguely familiar about the man but I can't put my finger on it. I'm pretty sure we never met while I was alive and although Lambert is a very common last name, I don't remember knowing anyone who could be related to the man.

Clothilde comes gliding up to Lambert. I had momentarily forgotten she was there with Evian stealing the show.

I hardly recognize her. She was never one to pay much attention to the rules of the physical realm but at least she mostly kept her human form. Her face is still Clothilde but her body is nothing but a blurry mass of gray. Her hair swirls around her head like it's a million little live serpents searching for their next victim.

And she's growing. When she reaches Lambert, she looms over him, almost entirely hiding him from my sight.

"You're going to pay," she says to him, her midnight voice lower and scarier than I've ever heard it.

Evian's breath catches and her hand trembles slightly when she lets go of Lambert's hand. Even Doubira seems to feel something and looks over his shoulder before shaking hands with Lambert.

"Clothilde," I say firmly. "You need to calm down or Evian and Doubira won't be able to do their job. If you want him to pay, they need to be able to focus."

We're here to help, but ghosts can't arrest live people.

It takes her a second or two, but Clothilde hears me. She moves away—not much, only a few paces, but it's enough for her to no longer be a distraction to Evian.

I move to stand by her side and put my hand where I estimate her shoulder should be. "I know you're angry, Clothilde. But you have to keep it together. We will only succeed if we stay calm and focused."

"I remember him." She's still using her midnight voice but the volume is on low. "He's the last thing I remember before waking up in my casket six feet under. He gave me a drink. And told me to follow him to his hotel room so he could get his suitcase."

Her eyes, as she turns to me, are pools of black, but it's not only anger I see in there. She's also scared. And lost.

"There's nothing you could have done differently," I tell her gently. "Once you tasted that drink, you were as good as dead. We'll get him now, okay? He'll pay for everything he's done. To you and to all those other girls."

Clothilde's eyes go back to normal. I think looking at me and turning her back on Lambert helps. Now I just need her to keep her emotions in check while Evian questions Lambert.

The introductions between Lambert and the police officers are done and Lambert is trying to convince Evian that he doesn't know Stéphane, that he doesn't understand why the man showed up in his office at all, and that therefore, the other man should go home.

"Quite clearly," he says in a haughty tone that implies he feels superior to everyone else in the room, "the man heard you say my name and decided to come investigate himself. You really should be careful with throwing names around like that, Captain Evian."

"He's right," Stéphane says, actually managing to catch onto what Lambert is hinting at. "When you said his name, I came here immediately to get answers about my old partner's death. I will not let his death go unavenged."

Okay, that's ridiculous. But unfortunately, it makes sense, and a judge or a jury could find it believable.

Evian doesn't even bother to argue. She's in charge here and I'm happy to see that she's not going to let someone like Lambert walk all over her. "You'll both stay. Would you like to talk here, Maître Lambert, or do you have a suitable office or meeting room somewhere?"

Lambert seems to realize there's no point in forcing the issue. He takes one step toward his office before changing his mind and leading the way to the meeting room he'd planned to push Stéphane into earlier.

"Mathieu," he says over his shoulder to the receptionist. "Why don't you take your sandwich outside today. I'll expect you back at two."

The poor man looks shell-shocked that his boss tells him to take a long lunch but he snaps out of it quickly and is out the door before we've all piled into the meeting room.

"We'd like to talk about Robert Villemur," Evian says.

FORTY-TWO

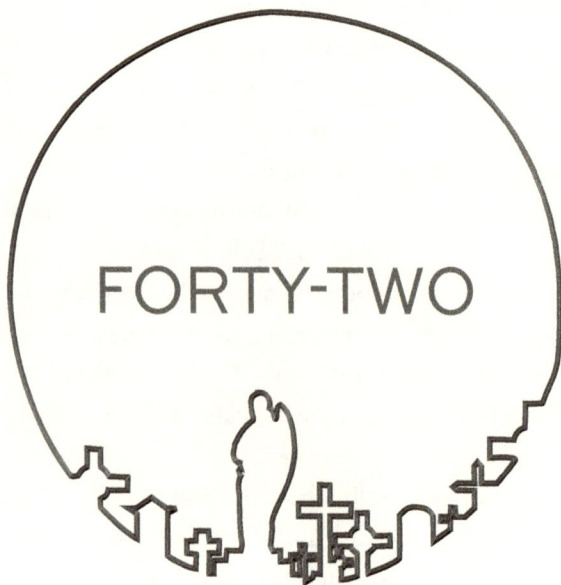

"I'M AFRAID YOU may have the wrong lawyer," Lambert says as he closes the meeting room door and takes a seat at the head of the oval table. "I cannot recall having a client named Robert Villemur. Or perhaps his case was handled by one of my colleagues?"

Evian and Doubira have both taken seats at the table, leaving two empty chairs between Evian and Lambert, but Stéphane is still standing. He hovers in the corner, wondering if he should sit next to Lambert or the police. In the end he goes with neither and sits two seats down from Lambert and across from Evian.

I've dragged Clothilde with me to the far side of the room, as far away from Lambert as possible. She seems to be in control of her emotions—but just barely.

"Oh, I do not believe Monsieur Villemur was a client," Evian says calmly. She's sitting straight in her chair, leaning slightly forward with her hands folded loosely on the table. I notice she has released the safety on the gun at her hip, which is a first. "He was a police officer who disappeared without a trace in 1988."

Lambert's eyebrows shoot up. "And you expect me to remember a police officer from over thirty years ago? Was he involved in a case that I worked on? I tend to forget the officers I meet in the context of my work but I never forget a client."

"There seems to be a link with Gérard de Villenouvelle. Him I assume you've heard of?"

Lambert takes a second too long to answer. He wanted to deny ever having heard of de Villenouvelle but realized that with the ongoing case against the man, that wouldn't have been credible for someone in his position.

Some emotion flickers across his face but I'm unable to catch it.

"I'm going to get closer to watch his reactions," I whisper to Clothilde. "Can you stay here by yourself?" I don't want her to get close to the man again but it might not be overly bright to say that out loud.

Clothilde seems to know it too, though. "Go," she says. "I'll watch from here."

I cross the room as Lambert makes his reply. "I've heard of the case," he says. "It's difficult not to hear of it in Toulouse these days. But he is not a client of mine."

"Really?" Evian turns a puzzled gaze to Doubira. "I could have sworn I saw Maître Lambert mentioned in the same report as one with de Villenouvelle's name in it."

Playing along, Doubira whips out his phone and opens a file. "One Laurent Lambert rented the hotel room where Clothilde Humbert was found dead in August 1988. The official charge hasn't been made yet since the finding is only days old, but de Villenouvelle's DNA was found on—actually *in*—Mademoiselle Humbert's body."

Evian nods and turns back to Lambert. "Do you often rent hotel rooms and then let shady police officers rape and murder people in them? Doesn't sound like a very smart thing to do for an upstanding citizen like yourself."

I'm close enough to observe every little twitch on Lambert's face. Right now, his nostrils flare the tiniest little bit and he's fighting the urge to flex his jaw. The man has very good control over his body's reactions. He just doesn't know that one of the people watching him is a ghost who's less than ten centimeters away.

"There have been occasions in the past where I have rented hotel rooms, apartments, cars—anything—for clients. My work is done with the utmost discretion and sometimes this means making sure there is no trace of my client's presence. This is never done to hide the client from the police, only to hide them from someone who wants to harm them."

"Which client did you rent that hotel room for in August 1988?" Evian asks.

His breathing has sped up a little but his shrug seems perfectly insouciant. "My memory is very good, Captain Evian, but surely you don't remember everything you did on a specific day thirty years ago."

"I was five in 1988, so no, I don't remember. But if a young girl was murdered in a hotel room *I* rented for someone else, it *would* stay with me for quite some time."

"Even though I rented the hotel room, that does not mean I knew what happened behind closed doors."

Evian turns to Doubira again. "Surely, the lawyer was at least interviewed?"

Doubira nods eagerly. "He gave a two-hour statement at the police station two days later. He had an alibi for the time of death, claimed to have not set foot in the place on the day of the murder."

Lambert extends his hands in a there-you-go gesture, as if this would make it perfectly normal for him to forget all about it.

Evian turns to Stéphane. "Why *did* you come here, so soon after our visit at your home?"

I decide to keep my eyes on Lambert. Now that all the live people in the room are looking at Stéphane, he'll believe he's unobserved.

He keeps his eyes on Evian. He couldn't care less about what reply Stéphane comes up with—he knows Evian is the real threat here. The fingers of his right hand twitch, as if wanting to fidget, and a muscle beneath his left eye jumps several times. He's nervous but he's going to be very hard to break.

"I, uh…" Stéphane trails off before even getting started on his answer. "I heard you say his name so I came to investigate."

"That's usually the job of the police. I believe you retired a decade ago?"

"Yes, yes…uh…it's just so ingrained, though. Following up on a lead is basically a reflex."

"And trusting your colleagues who are still in service isn't?" Evian's face is an impressively neutral mask. It's impossible to tell if she's actually insulted or not.

Lambert isn't very impressed with Stéphane's answers. I've caught one aborted eye roll and one slow and silent sigh. He stays silent and still to anyone not up in his face like I am, though.

"Uh…" I don't remember Stéphane ever being this out of it. Could be old age, I guess.

"How did you know where to find the right Laurent Lambert, by the way?" She turns to Doubira. "How many people with that name did we find in the White Pages?"

"Three in Toulouse," Doubira replies, without checking his phone this time.

Evian never takes her eyes of Stéphane, who I see literally squirming out of the corner of my eye.

Silence settles. I don't think Evian has any intention of breaking it.

This time it's Lambert's lips that twitch and he shoots a quick glance at Stéphane. He's worried what the old man might do.

Clothilde has kept her word and is still standing in the far corner. Her eyes are fixed on Lambert and I'm willing to bet she hasn't blinked once in the last ten minutes. With her shimmering form and black eyes, she would fit right into a horror movie.

As the silence stretches, even I become uncomfortable. I'm tempted to say something—anything—except nobody would actually hear me and it'd probably make an awkward situation even worse for everybody else.

"He told me to do it!" Stéphane says, his voice high and breathless. He's pointing a finger at Lambert.

"He told you to do what?" Evian asks.

"As your legal counsel," Lambert says in a strong voice that plows right over both the end of Evian's question and the beginnings of Stéphane's answer. "I recommend you don't say anything."

"Since when are you his lawyer?" Doubira asks. "That's one hundred percent contradictory to what you said ten minutes ago."

"Since right this moment," Lambert replies, eyes calm and empty as they stare down Doubira. "The man clearly needs a lawyer and I need some time with my new client before he answers any more of your questions."

I take one step away from Lambert so that I can also keep my eyes on Stéphane. He doesn't seem to know what to do with the current turn of events, his eyes darting from Lambert, to Evian, to the closed door.

Clothilde suddenly stands right behind Stéphane, hair moving, eyes pitch black, and body a mass of swirling gray. "Did you kill Robert?" she says in his ear, but loud enough that everybody can hear—those who are sufficiently sensitive to ghosts, anyway.

Seems like Stéphane is somewhat sensitive. He points a shaking finger at Lambert as he shoots out of his chair, making it topple to the floor behind him. "He told me to do it!"

My own partner pulled the trigger on me? Somehow, I'm not even surprised. I don't feel anger that he'd turn on me, or much of a sense of injustice at having my life cut short at thirty-five. It's shame that overwhelms everything else right in this moment.

I was bested by this idiot?

"Did Maître Lambert tell you to kill Robert Villemur?" Evian asks Stéphane, still calmly seated in her chair. Her eyes are on Stéphane but I'm willing to bet she'll jump into action if Lambert moves so much as a finger.

"Do not answer that question," Lambert says.

"*Bad* partner," Clothilde whispers into Stéphane's ear. The girl is becoming decidedly creepy.

Stéphane must agree because his stress levels clearly spike. He seems to have trouble breathing properly and it's just a question of time before he makes a run for it.

Except he doesn't run.

He shoves a hand inside his jacket.

"He has a gun!" I yell. The man shouldn't still be in possession of a gun if he's been retired for a decade but I recognize that move. He didn't like carrying his gun on his hip like everybody else. He kept yapping on about it when we were on a rare stakeout.

I don't know if Evian—or anyone—hears my warning, and it wouldn't have given them more than a second extra, anyway.

Stéphane pulls out his gun and points it at Evian.

FORTY-THREE

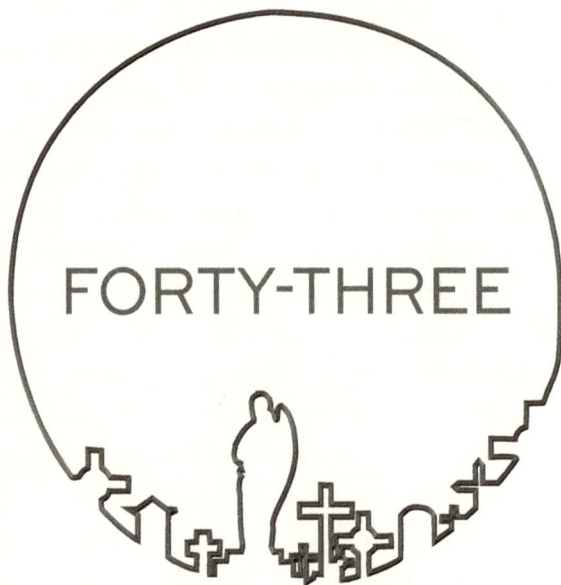

It's a good thing that Clothilde is standing behind Stéphane and is therefore one of the last people in the room to see the gun.

My first reaction is pure reflex, to throw myself at Stéphane. I'm close enough to perhaps be able to knock him down before he gets off a shot, or at the very least work as a human shield for the other people in the room.

Luckily, I remember that I don't have a physical body one step before hitting Stéphane. And I see the look and intention in Clothilde's gaze.

We're both going to crash into him.

"Clothilde, stop!" I yell and manage to change my course to go behind Stéphane's back and into Clothilde. I can't actually push her but she's so used to the two of us interacting that she moves back a step as if there was physical interaction.

"Don't mess with him," I whisper urgently. "He's not exactly mentally stable and *he has a loaded gun*. This is not the time to see if he's scared of ghosts." A nervous twitch and Evian could die.

At first Clothilde's expression is nothing but indignant anger at me cutting her off. In her current form, she's downright terrifying and I can hardly recognize my old friend. But she's still in there. And she hears what I'm saying. While Stéphane is still sputtering and the others remain motionless, she regains some of her usual shape and her eyes go back to normal.

"We can't just stand here and do nothing," she whispers.

"We won't," I promise her. "But we have to find the right time to intervene. At a point where an otherworldly distraction is a *good* thing."

I step to one side of Stéphane, finding a spot halfway through the table where I have a good view of everyone in the room, and Clothilde does the same on his other side. I can get to both Stéphane and Lambert easily, and Clothilde can get to Stéphane and Evian.

When Stéphane doesn't seem to have anything to say, Evian speaks up. "I take it you admit to killing Robert Villemur?"

"I didn't kill him! I put an end to his misery!"

Okay, I know my life was far from perfect but killing me to "put an end to my misery" is taking it a little far, surely?

"He was writhing on the floor and frothing at the mouth," Stéphane yells. "He was as good as dead and I took mercy on him." The gun wavers a little but it's still aimed at Evian. He's only three meters away from her—even Stéphane should be able to hit something at that distance.

"Why was he writhing on the floor and frothing at the mouth?" Evian asks. I have to admire her calm. Even police officers will be freaked out at having a gun pointed at them but it doesn't show in the least.

"Because of the poison." Stéphane waves his free hand in the air as if frustrated with everybody's incapacity to follow along. "I didn't give him the poison. But I had to sit with him until the end. And it took too damned long!"

I exchange a look with Clothilde. I was poisoned?

"Why did you have to sit with him?" Evian asks. "Why not take him to the hospital?"

Stéphane snorts in derision. "As if that would have done him any good. He got a quadruple dose to make sure it'd be quick."

"Who gave him the poison?"

"Who do you think?" When Evian doesn't offer a proposition, Stéphane jerks his head in Lambert's direction. "He's always been the one calling the shots."

I've been keeping an eye on Lambert but so far he hasn't moved a muscle since Stéphane pulled his gun. He hasn't had any reaction to anything Stéphane has said and doesn't seem overly bothered by the gun. Then again, it's not pointed at him.

Lambert stays cool in the face of this accusation. "I do not appreciate being accused of murder, Monsieur Petit. Unless you have proof, I suggest you retract your statement."

"I saw it! How's that for proof?"

"What exactly did you see, Monsieur Petit?"

"You gave Robert that cup of coffee! Ten minutes later he was spasming on the floor!"

"You saw me giving Monsieur Villemur a cup of coffee." Lambert leaves a pause for effect and he offers a sigh that sounds like a long-suffering one that he's doing his best to hold back. "I do not believe most people drop dead from drinking coffee."

Stéphane is still pointing the gun at Evian but most of his attention is on Lambert. I think that between the two of them, Doubira and Evian could take him out when he's so distracted but I suspect they choose not to. They want to see how this conversation plays out.

"You told me you were going to put something in that coffee," Stéphane insists. "Then I had to bring Robert to the back room so he wouldn't draw any attention. *Ten minutes!*"

"Monsieur Petit," Lambert says, and there's steel in his voice now. "Did you see me put poison in the coffee? Did you see what poison it might have been? Do you have any *proof*?"

"But that's…that's…you were *supposed* to— He couldn't— I *know* you did it!"

"Like I said, Monsieur Petit. I do not appreciate foundless accusations."

"They're not foundless!"

Stéphane's gun is no longer pointed at Evian. It's halfway to pointing at Lambert instead but I don't think he's doing it on purpose. I can't be certain since most of my focus is on Lambert and Stéphane, but I think both Evian and Doubira have their hands on their weapons.

Stéphane's panicked voice is about an octave higher than usual. "My accusations aren't *foundless* since they're the *truth*! You were going to poison Robert because he suddenly changed sides. Instead of being your lackey he decided to investigate the murder of Mademoiselle Grand and that wasn't in your plan."

Investigate? Had I decided to question the orders I'd been given?

I see no sign of nerves on Lambert. The man is made of ice. "Foundless accusations, Monsieur Petit. Find proof or stop talking. I may have to sue you for defamation—in front of the police, no less."

223

Uh oh. Stéphane is reminded that he's waving a gun in a room with two police officers. Except his gun is no longer pointed at them, it's now aimed at the unarmed lawyer.

Evian and Doubira saw it coming, though. They both had their guns in hand under the table and now swing them up to aim at Stéphane. "Put the gun down, Monsieur Petit," Evian says.

Weasel that he is, I honestly expect Stéphane to drop the gun. He was never the type to do well under pressure. A follower. A type I know well.

But he doesn't drop the gun. He firms his grip on the gun and points it directly at Lambert. "You drop your guns or I shoot the lawyer. He's the one you want here. You won't be able to solve your case if he's dead."

"Shooting a man will guarantee you a short life behind prison walls," Evian counters.

Stéphane shrugs. "I can't win this. The way I see it, my best case scenario is walking out of this building without handcuffs."

"And spend the rest of your days running?"

Shrug. "If I must. It's better than prison."

Evian sighs. "We cannot let you walk out, Monsieur Petit. You were a police officer. You *know* this."

"What I know is that I'm holding a gun to a presumed innocent civilian—who is also the guy you're after, you simply need to prove it—and saving his life is more important than making sure I don't walk free."

He has a point, dammit. If Lambert really is the brains behind the murders of dozens of young women going so far back as thirty years—and because of Clothilde I *know* this to be the case—then Evian can't afford for him to be killed, just to catch an old fart who pulled the trigger on a dying cop.

Clothilde sidles up next to me and asks me in a whisper, "Will they be able to get Lambert after that confession?"

I shake my head. "They can bring him in for questioning and hold him for forty-eight hours. But if they don't find some sort of proof, he'll be free to go. Everybody is presumed innocent until proven otherwise, remember?"

"But I *know* he's the one who killed *me*."

"I know. But ghosts don't work so well as witnesses."

"We can't let your partner get away," she says. "*He* can work as a witness. He's our best chance in getting at Lambert."

"You're right." I move us both next to Stéphane. "I think Evian will pick up on it if we do something. But Stéphane is a lot less attuned to us, so we have to be loud, all right?"

Clothilde flashes an evil grin. "I can be loud. What are we aiming for?"

"Distraction," I say. "We need to confuse Stéphane so that Doubira and Evian can take him down. And so that he doesn't kill anyone in the process."

Evian gives us the opening we need almost immediately. "You win, for now, Monsieur Petit. We'll put our weapons down if you promise to walk out without harming anyone."

When both police officers start lowering their guns, Stéphane's attention is split between the guns and Lambert, who he's still pointing his gun at.

"Now!" I yell at Clothilde and jump on Stéphane, screaming my head off.

Clothilde follows suit.

FORTY-FOUR

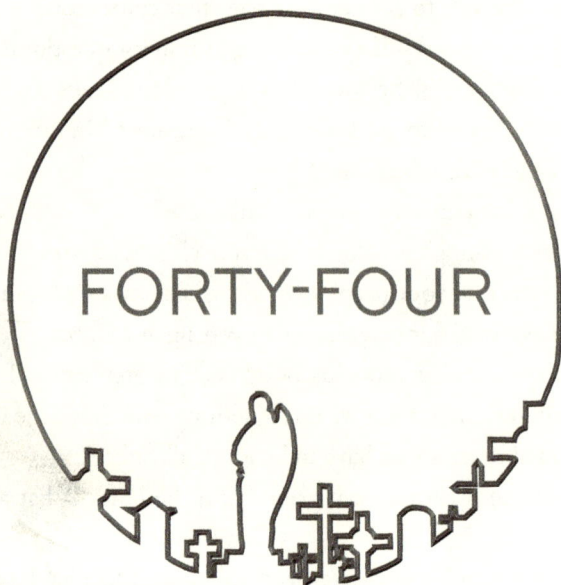

NOTHING GOES AS expected. But at the same time...Emeline is somehow not surprised when Petit jumps as if scared of something invisible, his eyes bulging and mouth opening in horror.

And arms flailing.

He still holds the gun but it's not aimed at Lambert anymore. It's pointed somewhere between the door and the ceiling.

Emeline abandons the action of putting her gun down and instead aims it straight at Petit. In her peripheral vision, she's happy to see Malik doing the same thing.

"Put the gun down, Monsieur," she says in her most commanding voice.

Petit seems to be fighting with what Emeline would qualify as voices in his head, his eyes darting wildly from side to side as if trying to catch a glimpse of whatever he's imagining, but his grip on the gun is still firm.

And when Emeline speaks, his gaze focuses back on her.

His arm lowers, the gun's aim approaching Emeline.

"Put the gun down or we *will* shoot," Malik warns. His voice is solid, as is his aim.

Petit doesn't put the gun down.

He aims his gun at Emeline.

The hand holding the gun wavers a little and his left hand goes up to cover his ear. This man is seriously deranged. He should *not* be carrying a gun, especially one that seems to be a service gun. Why does he still have it?

"Monsieur—"

Malik doesn't get more than one word out before Petit firms his grip on the gun and crooks his finger on the trigger.

He's going to bloody shoot.

Malik gets there first. Without hesitation, he aims for Petit's leg and pulls the trigger.

Emeline throws herself to the floor. Chances are Petit will follow through on his action.

A second bang goes off.

Petit fired his shot.

While she's still falling, Emeline *feels* the air of the bullet flying past her head.

On the floor—alive and ears ringing—Emeline keeps her grip on her gun and aims it toward Petit under the table and office chairs.

Petit's gun drops to the floor at his feet. Then the rest of the man follows; first one knee on the ground, then his rear, and finally his head and shoulders. He's clutching at his left thigh, where blood is already coloring his pants, spreading out in all directions.

Malik makes a quick call on the radio, calling for backup and an ambulance.

Emeline decides to keep her gun on Petit while Malik approaches to relieve the man of his gun and to put him in handcuffs. Except, suddenly, she feels the need to touch her head, where the bullet sped past a short moment earlier.

Her hand comes away bloody.

Ah, looks like the shot was a little closer than she thought.

She touches the wound again, trying to judge the quantity of blood pouring out. It doesn't seem like a hemorrhage, although head wounds always bleed a lot. The left part of her jacket is already soaked.

Malik, swearing, brings Emeline's focus back where it should be—on their suspect. Emeline places her left hand where she thinks her head wound is and pushes down as hard as she can. It will have to suffice until the ambulance gets here.

Malik is bent over Petit but not to put him in handcuffs. He's making a tourniquet around Petit's wound, his movements ragged and hurried.

Why hasn't he first secured the suspect? And the gun is still lying there, within reach.

Emeline crawls around the table on one hand and two knees, her left hand continuing to push down on her own wound. She wants to get to the gun and then have a talk with Malik on priorities.

She never makes it to the gun. When she comes around the table and Malik no longer hinders her view of Petit, her direction changes and she goes straight for the old man now lying prone on the floor.

"What happened?" she asks. She grabs for Petit's neck, looking for a pulse, but it's complicated because her hands are slippery with blood.

"I think I hit the main artery," Malik says, his voice terse and clipped. His eyes are on his task, dark and focused, and the muscles of his jaw jump at regular intervals. "Now I think he's having a heart attack."

Oh, no, he won't. He's not getting away that easily.

Emeline lets go of her own wound, bleeding be damned. She dries off one hand on her leg and tries again for a pulse. She *might* have felt one beat but she's not even sure.

"I'm doing CPR," she says and opens Petit's shirt to make sure his airways are clear and to do the CPR directly on his chest. As he lies there, she's reminded of how old this man is. They shot a man in his mid-seventies.

They keep working on reviving Stéphane Petit until the paramedics show up. Lambert has apparently let them into the building but other than that, Emeline has no idea what the lawyer's been up to since the shots were fired.

The paramedics take over, their machines much more effective than Emeline and Malik with their bare hands.

Emeline doesn't feel too confident it will be enough, though.

She moves away to sit with her back against the meeting room wall, wanting some calm to collect her thoughts but one of the paramedics, a small black woman with startlingly blue eyes, follows her with bandages and God knows what else in hand.

"Will you let me look at your wound, officer?" The paramedic doesn't wait for an answer and starts applying something to Emeline's hair.

"It's nothing serious," she says but lets the woman do her job.

"I know." Her smile is kind and wide. "But you're bleeding a fountain and I think it's best if we don't scare the shit out of the civilians you're bound to run into when you go back outside. Besides, even if the wound itself isn't serious, if you lose enough blood, that can become a problem."

Emeline enjoys the attention during this short little break.

Lambert is still there. He's staying out of the way, leaning against the wall not far from the door, his hands in his pants pockets and a perfectly neutral expression on his dignified face as he observes everything. His eyes meet Emeline's across the room and though his face doesn't really change at all, Emeline gets his message loud and clear.

She has nothing on him and her key witness was just rushed out of the building on a gurney.

He's going to a walk free.

FORTY-FIVE

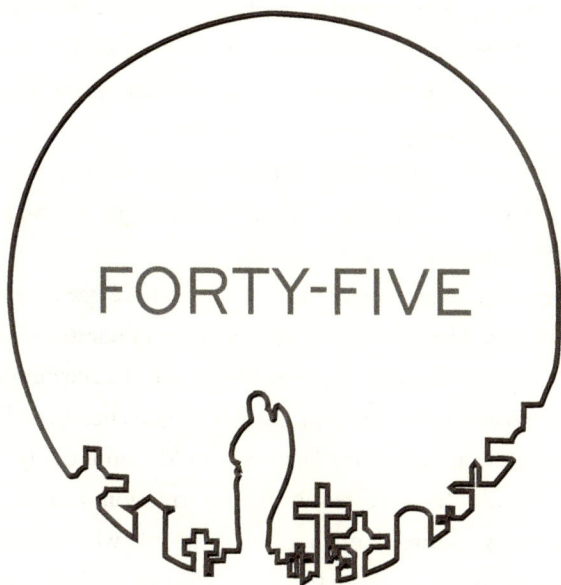

STÉPHANE ISN'T GOING to make it.

Clothilde and I both hover over Evian and Doubira as they do CPR and then over the paramedics when they arrive. We try to not step *through* anyone, in case they're sensitive enough to be bothered by it but I'm not entirely certain we succeed. In any case, everybody is focused on the dying man on the floor.

"What happens if he dies?" Clothilde asks, her eyes laser sharp and her mouth in a thin line. "Does what he said still count as a testimony against Lambert?" She hovers with her face mere centimeters from Stéphane's chest, looking for signs of a breath or a heartbeat.

231

I sigh. "They can put it in the report and it will go on record—but it's not going to be enough to put away someone like Lambert." It wouldn't be enough to put away *anyone*, except if the testimony made the other guy freak out and admit everything.

Lambert certainly won't admit a thing.

We watch the paramedics work for another minute, pushing air into Stéphane's lungs and using machines to jump-start his heart. They move him onto a gurney.

"Even if he lived, I don't think it would have been enough to get to someone like Lambert," I say. The man in question has been standing in a corner observing everything since the beginning. He doesn't seem affected in the least, neither by guns being fired inside his meeting room, nor by the fact that an old man is dying.

"We could have gotten more information out of him," Clothilde says. "More clues about other people who could help."

I shrug. It's a setback, but not a big one. I'm convinced Stéphane wouldn't have helped us much anyway. In fact, the whole process of questioning him, of preparing his trial, of running after people he knew but who were surely not much more important than him in the large scheme of things, would just have taken up a lot of the police's time.

"The man has been involved in dozens of murders," I say to Clothilde. "We know about several of the victims and have names galore of people we need to look into. We're not exactly lacking in leads."

As the paramedics strap Stéphane onto the gurney, Clothilde bends down to pretty much shove her nose into Stéphane's neck. "I think he's turning into a ghost." She looks up at me. "Is that possible?"

I join her at the gurney, ignoring the fact that I completely cover a short woman making sure one of the machines is securely attached. I bend down to look.

There's a faint shimmer. Something white or gray, just below or running along the surface of Stéphane's skin.

"He's already turning into a ghost," Clothilde says with awe. In our cemetery, we only saw people emerge as ghosts after several days underground. But this is the first time we've been outside in the real world when someone passed away.

"The first thing I remember is from being trapped in the casket," I say.

"I was aware of things happening around me during short periods," Clothilde says. "I wasn't completely in control of my mind until I was properly buried, though. I've never heard of anyone else that happened to. Maybe the ghost is always there from the start? It's just that everybody don't remember, or don't come to at all until they're under ground?"

"I guess it's possible."

I keep my eyes glued to the shimmer on Stéphane. It *does* have the color and consistency, if that's the right word to use, of most ghosts. It looks sort of solid but at the same time it's sort of translucent.

"What's going on?"

I jump back with a yell when Stéphane screams the question. Clothilde's reaction is much the same.

It's Stéphane's voice but his mouth didn't move. Not the real one and not the ghost one.

Clothilde leans back down to speak in Stéphane's ear. "Are you dead?"

I swallow a laugh at the oddness of the situation. "Stéphane?" I say. "Can you hear us?"

"Of course I can hear you! But I can't see a bloody thing. And I can't move. What the hell is going on? How can this be legal?"

Okay, it's definitely not the live body of Stéphane who's talking, so we're going to go with the hypothesis of him being a ghost.

Apparently stuck in his own body at the moment, to the point of being blind.

I take a few seconds to think about how to present this to Stéphane. How do you convince someone they're dead? And with the paramedics picking up their stuff, I don't think we have much time.

Stéphane speaks first. "Who— What's going— I know that voice. But that's not— I saw you die with my own eyes! I put a bullet through your heart!"

"Nice to see you again, too, Stéphane." This reunion is a lot less satisfactory than I'd have thought. "I'm afraid you're right, though. I did die. In fact, I've been a ghost for thirty years."

I share a look with Clothilde—we've had a lot of odd conversations with new ghosts over the years but I do believe this takes the cake.

"And if you can hear us now," I continue, my voice taking on a gleeful tone that I'm not even going to apologize for, "it means you're a ghost too! Welcome to the other side."

Clothilde is bent over in silent laughter, her wavy hair dancing with mirth and eyes alight with mischief.

"You're a— But that can't be—" There's a break, where I assume Stéphane tries to take a calming breath—except breaths don't change anything when you're a ghost. "Are you holding me captive?"

"What? No, of course not." I snort a laugh. "Ghosts don't have corporeal forms. We can pretend to touch each other but you'll never actually feel the touch of anything or anyone ever again."

Okay, that took a dark turn.

I shake out of it, and continue. "I've never actually seen someone become a ghost before but I think you'll only be let out once you accept you're a ghost. And that's a lot easier when you've spent a couple of days banging on your casket, trying to get out. Fun times, you'll see."

The gurney starts to move and I move with them. Evian is still on the floor, talking to Doubira, so I only have until Stéphane is moved out of the office. "Seriously, though, Stéphane, I need your help. We're on a schedule here and we need all the information you have on Lambert. That man needs to pay for everything he's done.

"You owe me this much," I add. "After pulling the trigger on your own partner, it's honestly the least you could do."

"I'm really sorry about that," Stéphane says, his voice small. "I didn't have a choice."

Clothilde snorts but keeps quiet. We don't want to waste any time on Stéphane wondering who she is.

"There's always a choice," I say, feeling like a cliché.

"You were as good as dead already, Robert. The poison they gave you was really strong and you were in a lot of pain. You could say it was a mercy shot."

"You could have called for help but decided instead to put a bullet through my heart, Stéphane."

"And I've regretted that choice every day of my life." Stéphane makes a noise that might have been an attempt at a sigh—again, a learned skill when you no longer have lungs. "I was scared and young. They told me you would die anyway and that if I didn't do as they said, they would come after me *and* my family. They promised me a lot of money. I took it."

We're getting dangerously close to the outer door of Lambert's office and I'm not sure if we'll be able to follow once they pass through.

"About Lambert—"

"I've always wanted to apologize to you, Robert," Stéphane says. "I'm sorry, all right? I did the wrong thing and messed up big time." A short pause. "I'm ready to pay for my sins."

A ripple runs through the shimmer on Stéphane's skin, then the whole thing blinks out.

The paramedics push the gurney through the door, closing the door behind them, making it impossible for us to follow.

"Did he just move on?" Clothilde asks. "Was his unfinished business with you and he got it over with before even being declared dead? That's so unfair!"

I agree with the sentiment but what's more important is that Stéphane is now beyond our reach.

Lambert is going to walk.

FORTY-SIX

EVIAN AND DOUBIRA spend almost two days finishing their report. It's not on the murders of dozens of young girls spanning over three decades. It's not on the murder of Clothilde Humbert, or even Gisèle Grand. It's on the disappearance and murder of one Robert Villemur.

Since I had been involved in the investigation of the murder of Gisèle Grand, she is also mentioned, and Evian recommends for someone to reopen the case to look for links with the ongoing trial of Gérard de Villenouvelle. I hope whoever gets that case will be able to bring some closure to Gisèle's sister.

The report mentions Maître Laurent Lambert exactly once, to list him as a witness to Stéphane's confession.

Evian was nice enough to proofread the whole report on paper, letting us ghosts read over her shoulder. I'm pretty sure she did it on purpose, though not quite consciously.

This morning, Evian and Doubira march into Diome's office, closing the door behind them, to officially hand over the report.

The man still towers over everyone, Doubira included, but nothing in his manner is intimidating. He invites Evian and Doubira to have a seat and he even has a cup of coffee for Doubira and a cup of tea for Evian at the ready. The poor plant on his desk is looking even worse than the last time we were here, its leaves hanging limply over the rim of its pot.

"Lieutenant Robert Villemur is officially a hero who died in service to our country," Evian says as she pushes the folder across the desk toward Diome.

I *know* that isn't exactly true. I know it's the way they present it so that the police will look good and so that the big boss will be happy. Attempting—and failing—to fix your own mistakes doesn't make you a hero.

And yet, somehow, it changes everything.

Someone thinks I did the right thing. That I did something worthwhile. There's an official document that will make it go down in history that I was a *good* guy.

It might be pathetic but it makes me happy.

I did something right.

"This is what Madame Spangero wanted?" Evian adds after a second's pause.

Diome pats the report but doesn't open it. He already received an electronic copy of one of the earlier drafts.

His words are measured when he replies to Evian. "We do not solve cases to do as anyone wants, no matter which position they occupy."

Evian gives a perfunctory smile. "I didn't say what the report says is wrong. I would never do that, even if it means losing my job. But the *scope* of this report is somewhat different from what you brought me down here from Paris to do."

Diome raises one meaty finger from the folder. "But there is a link between the two. This was merely the first step in a much larger case."

"Is that how you're presenting it to Spangero? Does this mean I'm staying in Toulouse?"

"For the time being, yes, I would like for you to stay here a while longer. Even this report makes it clear that at least two officers—Villemur and Petit—were corrupt while working the cases of assumed suicides. As long as we cannot ascertain that they were the only two, anyone local is a suspect."

Evian glances at Doubira, who is, in fact, a local.

"I have taken the liberty of assuming Doubira is clean," Diome says gravely, "as he was still in school when the most recent murders were perpetrated. It is not possible for one person to work a case such as this alone."

"True," Evian says with the beginnings of a smile. She's running a finger along the rim of her cup of tea but has yet to take a sip. "I have much appreciated Doubira's help on this case and hope I'll be allowed to bring him along for whatever comes next?"

"Certainly," Diome says then turns to face Doubira. "If young Doubira agrees to the mission?"

As Doubira takes a couple of seconds to reply, I really look at him for the first time since we entered the room. He's sitting straight as usual, his clothes clean and neatly ironed. He's drunk about half his coffee already and is holding the little cup in his large hands in his lap.

Hands that are a little too tense for simply holding a cup of coffee.

He licks his lips and forces a smile that doesn't quite reach his eyes. "Of course I'd like to continue working with Evian on this case. Someone has to make sure those young women find justice."

Diome nods. "How are you feeling these days, Doubira? Sleeping well?"

Doubira gulps. "I'm fine, thanks."

"You were involved in an altercation where a man lost his life." Diome's low voice is calming and trust-inspiring. I like this man. He's the kind of man I'd have done well to follow back in the day and would be proud to work beside today. "This was the first time you fired your weapon outside of training, yes?"

Doubira gulps and nods.

"There is no shame in having feelings, Monsieur Doubira. In fact, I would go so far as to say it would be a bad sign if you were indifferent. But there is no doubt that you made the right choice of action. The lives of three persons were at stake."

Doubira nods again but doesn't lift his eyes from his cup.

"I will make certain you are set up for as many meetings with our psychologist as you need," Diome says. His words and tone are kind but it's also clear that this is not something Doubira will be allowed to refuse.

Diome turns back to Evian. "There is one element missing from your report."

Evian's eyebrows jump up. "Is that so?"

Leaning back in his chair, making the poor thing scream in protest, Diome folds his large hands in his lap. "We still do not know why Monsieur Villemur was buried next to Mademoiselle Humbert. We do not know *who* buried him. And we do not know—officially—who poisoned him. If, indeed, he was poisoned."

He's asking her to look into Laurent Lambert. Not directly, since he hasn't mentioned the man by name and the lawyer is in no way presented as a bad guy in the report. But in this room, we all know he was the poisoner.

"Spangero will be on board with me looking into this?" Evian asks.

"Spangero does not run this police station. I do. She may give guidelines but I will not allow for her to stop an important investigation without grounds."

Does that mean he thinks she *has* grounds for stopping us from investigating the murders of the young women?

Evian finally takes a sip of her tea, although it doesn't seem to be to her taste. She fiddles with the bracelet, turning it around her wrist several times, making my little finger tingle.

"I will investigate the link between Robert Villemur and Clothilde Humbert," she says. "Will you expect frequent or detailed reports?"

Diome shakes his head. "I trust you, Evian. Simply let me know if you need my assistance in any way."

So he doesn't want to be in the loop, probably to make sure Spangero won't have an excuse to stop them again. Should get interesting.

Clothilde, who has spent the entire meeting perched on a low cabinet at the back of the office, speaks up. "So now that you're officially a hero, can we finally look into my case? You think I'll be a hero too?"

"I'm sure you will be," I tell her with a huge grin. And we're going to be there with Evian, every step of the way.

FORTY-SEVEN

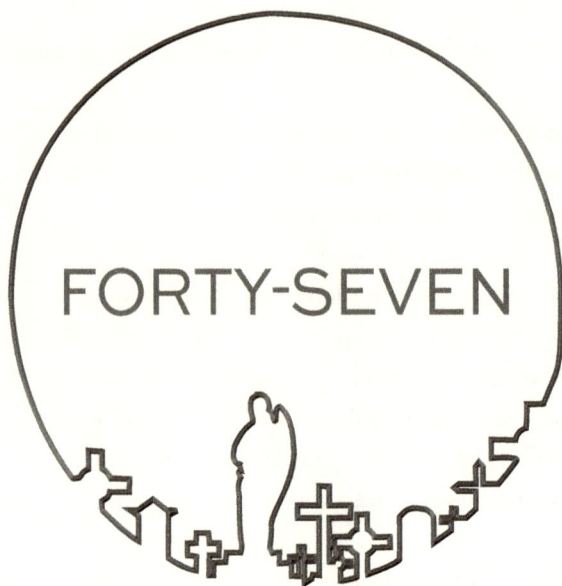

THE DAY IS warm enough for Evian to forego her jacket. She's wearing her usual jeans, boots and a simple, white t-shirt that she's already starting to sweat through. Doubira is clothed much the same but he doesn't seem to be having any trouble with the heat. His step is light although the worry that has been etched between his eyebrows since he shot Stéphane is ever-present.

We're back at the cemetery. *Our* cemetery.

It feels odd to see it from the outside. Everything is just a little different, seen from a new and different angle. The sun reflects off the bronze church roof in a glare that I never experienced from inside the walls. The wall around the cemetery looks gray and sad and stark from the outside, whereas the inside was covered in green growth almost from one end to the other.

Some things are still the same, of course. The wisteria along the north wall is in full bloom and the large leaves of the plane trees along the main path are creating comfortable shadows for visitors, bidding us welcome. The usual graves have fresh flowers—I see both roses on the Valentin tomb and chrysanthemums on the Fabre grave—and it looks like there's been a new burial since we left. A wooden cross stands at the head of a rectangle of fresh dirt.

I don't see any new ghosts, so I hope the poor soul got to move on directly instead of lingering here, all alone in the cemetery.

"What if I can't get back out?" Clothilde says nervously by my shoulder. "What if I get stuck here again?" We're hovering by Evian's little rental while Evian gets something from the trunk.

Clothilde *never* shows nervousness. That's not her style. And although I'd love to make fun of her for worrying now, I can't bring myself to do it. She's my best friend and genuinely worried and there's no choice for me but to reassure her.

"You managed to separate from your body in the hospital, you can do it again. As long as Evian has that one bone on her, you'll be able to follow." At least, that's what I'm banking on. Because I don't want to lose Clothilde, either.

"What if she decides to throw away the finger bones?" Clothilde insists, her clear eyes widening and one hand running through her hair.

I shush her. "Don't say that out loud and put any ideas in her head." Evian and Doubira walk toward the cemetery gate and as I trail after them, I sign for Clothilde to follow. "Come on, let's keep talking to her and tell her to *keep* the bones."

The thing is, if Evian dumps the bones, we'll both be stuck here. The rest of my body might still be in a morgue somewhere, but since I'm in no way close to it, I'm stuck with the finger bone.

Clothilde, on the other hand, will need to decide to follow the one bone that can leave this cemetery after our visit, and not the rest of her body, which is now back in its grave. She did it once, so I trust she can do it again, but if she needs reassurance, I'll give it.

It feels odd to be back to the place we haunted for thirty years. We've been away mere weeks, but it feels much longer.

This cemetery was my home for a long time, and I was happy here. But it's in the past now. My future is out in the world, helping Evian with solving the case of mine and Clothilde's murders.

As we approach the area toward the back gate where Clothilde's grave is, I notice something else that is new. "They've put your whole name on the gravestone, Clothilde."

Clothilde runs off ahead of us, bending at the waist as if she needs to be a mere hand's breadth away from the granite to read the freshly engraved golden letters. It not only has her first and last names, but also date of birth *and* date of death.

Clothilde straightens and dons a bored expression as if unbothered by the new discovery but I know she's touched. She never said anything, but being the only one with nothing but a first name and a date of death on her headstone never sat well with her.

Evian opens the bag she brought with her from the car. She'd emerged from her bedroom with it in hand this morning, so I don't know what's in it. Apparently something for Clothilde.

"I have no idea if this would actually fit," Evian says to the headstone. "And I wish I could have given it to you before they buried you again, but I'm thinking late is better than never. I haven't worn them in over twenty years and won't be needing them anytime soon." She empties the content of the bag on Clothilde's grave, one item at a time. First, a white blouse. Then, a worn pair of jeans. And finally, a pair of red Converse.

Clothilde stares at the clothes, her mouth hanging open and her hands going toward them by their own accord. "How did she get everything right?" she whispers. "She's never seen us."

I'm as speechless as Clothilde. Evian has brought her her go-to ensemble, the one she's the most comfortable with. The one that fits her so much better than the horrid yellow dress she was buried in.

Clothilde's eyes leave the clothes to land on Evian, filled to the rim with gratitude and hero-worship. "You even got the color of the shoes right. How did you do that? Even I haven't seen their color in thirty years."

I glance at the shoes and a smile stretches across my face as I mentally insert their color into all my memories of Clothilde perching on tombstones and letting her Converse-clad feet swing through the stone.

Evian glances around her—or maybe looks up at Clothilde, nothing would surprise me right now—then says, pretending it's for Doubira, "I wasn't actually sure about the shoe color, but from what we've learned, she seemed the kind to like the red ones."

"How do you even know this is how she dressed?" Doubira asks.

Evian shrugs. "Someone must have mentioned it to me."

Nobody mentioned anything to her. We've been with her every moment of every day since we left the morgue, and unless she's been having meetings in her bedroom at night, we've witnessed everything she has done on this case. There was no mention of clothes.

Doubira seems to accept the explanation and the pair fall into silence. They stand there for several minutes, each lost in their own thoughts.

I take the opportunity to make a quick tour of the cemetery, to say goodbye. I suspect we won't be coming back anytime soon, and I hadn't realized that fact the last time we left. I let my fingers run through the wisteria, give a pat to the graves of some old friends who've moved on ages ago, and smile at the sparrows searching for food on the area in front of the church.

When I rejoin the others, Evian and Doubira are getting ready to go. The clothes stay on the grave and will probably be picked up by someone during a visit in less than a day. The idea that they're even temporarily with Clothilde's body pleases me, nonetheless.

We follow Evian closely as she approaches the gate toward the parking lot. I can see Clothilde focusing all her mental energy on the bracelet on Evian's wrist.

"Get as close as you can," I tell her. If Evian somehow manages to exit the cemetery without Clothilde, it will already be too late for her to stay connected to the finger bone.

Clothilde goes all out and stands *inside* Evian. I can barely see my friend as she disappears into the larger woman's body.

Evian gives a full-body shiver and stops walking. Then she firms her jaw, cocks her head, and powers foward. It looks like she's walking against the wind in a full storm.

They make it to the gate, which Doubira is holding open.

Evian places one foot on the outside and stops.

Doubira looks at her oddly, but Clothilde doesn't miss a beat. She steps through the gate and out of the cemetery.

"Thank you," she says to Evian.

Evian nods and resumes walking normally toward the car as if nothing happened. "Do you want to drive, Malik?" she throws over her shoulder.

Clothilde grins, and just like that, we're ready for new adventures.

Ready to get justice.

AUTHOR'S NOTE

THANK YOU FOR reading *Beyond the Grave*. I hope you enjoyed it! I certainly had a blast writing it.

As you can see, this isn't over. One guy is in jail, but all the others are still running free. Unacceptable! So naturally, this series will have several more installments. No cliffhangers and every book can stand by itself, but there will also be the overarching plot of Robert and Clothilde seeking justice for themselves.

I hope you'll want to join me in the continuation of their story! The next story is called *Unveiling the Past* and is already available for preorder.

If you haven't tried out the *Ghost Detective* short stories yet, the first one (the one that started it all!) is available for free for my newsletter subscribers. You'll find the signup form on my website.

R. W. Wallace
www.rwwallace.com

ABOUT THE AUTHOR

R. W. WALLACE WRITES in most genres, though she tends to end up in mystery more often than not. Dead bodies keep popping up all over the place whenever she sits down in front of her keyboard.

The stories mostly take place in Norway or France; the country she was born in and the one that has been her home for two decades. Don't ask her why she writes in English—she won't have a sensible answer for you.

Her Ghost Detective short story series appears in *Pulphouse Magazine*, starting in issue #9.

You can find all her books, long and short, all genres, on rwwallace.com.

Also by R.W. Wallace

Mystery

Ghost Detective Novels
Beyond the Grave
Unveiling the Past
Beneath the Surface

Ghost Detective Shorts
Just Desserts
Lost Friends
Family Bonds
Common Ground
Till Death
Family History
Heritage
Eternal Bond
New Beginnings
Severed Ties

The Tolosa Mystery Series
The Red Brick Haze
The Red Brick Cellars
The Red Brick Basilica

Short Story Collections
Deep Dark Secrets
A Thief in the Night

Short Stories
Cold Blue Eternity
Hidden Horrors

Printed in the USA
CPSIA information can be obtained
at www.ICGtesting.com
JSHW080937200823
46844JS00001B/56

9 791095 707585